PORK CHOPS OF DEATH

A Zolly Mystery

BY FRANK MULA

First Edition: October 2013
Printed in the US

Thrown Free Books
ISBN 978-1-62217-027-2

CHAPTER ONE

You can smell murder. It lingers in the air like charged atoms after a bolt of lightning. It prickles the hairs inside your nostrils. I smelled it that day on the boardwalk.

I'm Zolly. Yeah I know, strange name, but it could be worse. You see I'm the product of a peculiarly American tradition of naming children - the ethnic car crash. Let's call Dad's Italians the Fiats, and Mom's Hungarians the Buicks. I know, they don't make Buicks in Hungary, but they don't make anything famous in Hungary except goulash. And no offense, but a lot of my Hungarian aunts resemble Buicks.

So one day my folks fall in love and BAM! The Fiat runs a stop light and back-ends the Buick, creating me - sort of a "Fuick." Now when it came to naming the little accident my parents had good intentions, but the farsightedness of snails. Mom chose "Zoltan" to please the Hungarians. My Dad contributed our Italian last name, Michelangelo. You see, I told you it could be worse, and it is. Zoltan Michelangelo.

God how I cursed them when I was struggling to write my name in kindergarten. How I envied Ed Fox and Wu Ho. My first scribbled essay in second grade was about the death of my parents in a car crash, and my subsequent adoption by the Ho family.

But I survived, and forty-two years later I like to recall what my Uncle Jerome always said when people asked how he was doing. "Abbastanza buono," he'd say with a shrug. Translated that means "good enough." I always liked that. Yeah, I'm doing "good enough." I like my job, and I'm living at my favorite place in the world - the Jersey Shore. More specifically, I'm in a pre-war fourplex a couple of blocks off the boardwalk at Seaside Heights.

To me there's no place else on earth like the boardwalk. On one side I've got a picture postcard of waves crashing romantically on a sandy beach - they've pretty much cleared up the problem of hypodermics and other medical waste washing in with the tide. On the other side are the wheels of fortune where I can win cute furry animals the Chinese have stuffed with toxic waste. I've also got stands serving the sustenance of a bachelor's life: caramel corn, fudge, pizza, sausage and pepper sandwiches, and my favorite - zeppoles. Zeppoles are golden globs of pizza dough deep fried and sprinkled with powdered sugar while sizzling hot.

It was on one of my daily boardwalk "fitness" walks that I found myself munching a three bagger and watching the gulls diving into the ocean after their dinner. Side note: If reincarnation is real and anyone gives you the choice, remember it's better to be a fish than a gull. Everybody in this life gets eaten, but at least the fish don't see it coming.

I didn't see it coming either, but I felt it. *Smelled it.* Something foul was behind me, getting closer.

"Hey YOU!" I felt a sudden heavy chop across my shoulder blade and a meaty paw grab my arm. I spun on my heels ready to stare death in the eye, but my scowl quickly softened when I found myself looking at a familiar face. Actually it was more wrinkles and wisps of gray hair than face. They belonged to Blinks, one of the harmless old rummies who drifted around town. He blinked like two hundred times per second as he stared at me with his neediest face. "Hey you remember your pal, don't ya? Got something for your pal?"

"Shit," I said to myself, handing him the bag with the remaining zeppole. Alright, I'm a sucker. But they say charity is good for the soul. And maybe this would keep Blinks from stealing the lawn furniture off my porch again. Blinks peered down into the bag and a look of indignation crossed his face.

"Cholesterol will kill ya, Shorty," he snorted taking a bite of one of my lost beauties and shambling off.

What the hell?! Talk about biting the hand that feeds you. "Shorty?" C'mon. I walked to the business side of the boardwalk to examine my dapper self in a mirror outside a shop selling sunglasses. I'm the first to admit I'm no N.B.A. center, but I'm at least 5'11. All right, to be 5'11 I wouldn't need lifts in my shoes, I'd need an Otis elevator. Let's say I'm 5'8 and remain friends.

But not a bad looking moke, I was forced to admit as I stared at my image in the glass. I adjusted the tilt of my plaid London Fog fedora so the red feather in the band proclaimed my feistiness like a bold "number one!" Yeah it was July, but I always wear a hat. My dad wore a hat. A hat makes you look like a gentleman. A hat protects you from the rain and sun. A hat makes you look two inches taller.

Wiping the last zeppole grease off my mitts I found myself behind a gaggle of girls wearing bikinis so brief they looked like they were stapled on. Did I tell you I love the Jersey Shore? But enough. Any more and I'll have to go to confession. And I haven't been to confession since our monsignor hit his lotto number and moved to Mykonos to tend to the troubled rich and famous. The new young priest from India seemed to take a little too much vicarious pleasure from my sins to suit my taste.

My power walk ended at a white clapboard building slumping toward the boardwalk and peeling about twenty-five coats of white enamel. The Chatterbox. It was your typical Jersey bar and grill. If these walls could talk, they'd mumble incoherently. They say Springsteen played here when he was a kid, but I'm guessing it was most likely Mozart.

Inside the bar was dark and smelled of old shoes. Or it might have been spilt beer. At the Chatterbox there wasn't much difference. I threaded my way through a tangle of chrome and Formica tables and at the back pushed through a squeaky swinging door. I found myself inside a storage room lined with iron shelves hugging the walls precariously. They were stacked with all the essentials of bar keeping – pickled eggs, beer nuts, and cans of that cat litter-like stuff you throw on vomit.

In the center of the room a hot blonde sat at a rickety card table shuffling a deck of Tarot cards. She had legs so long they seemed to go right through floor; and the black satiny blouse of her barmaid outfit pinched her cleavage into an erotic Grand Canyon. "Oh, hey," she said, finally acknowledging me with a quick glance.

"Hey," I shot back.

"Take a seat," she said, so I did. As she concentrated on the cards her lips curled up thinly. The long plastic earrings dangling from her earlobes framed the upturned lips and caused her face to resemble a smiling goal post. She finished dealing the cards then with a wary sigh began turning them over, each card providing a glimpse into my future. "Ah. I see a woman in your life. A tall woman... Oh yes, this woman definitely wants something from you."

"What does she want?" I asked. Suddenly I felt the toe of her shoe poke up under my pant cuff and wrap around my ankle as if doing a sexy pole dance.

"She wants... to go dancing!"

"Oh Hell," I moaned. "C'mon Tina, not the dancing thing again."

"C'mon yourself, Zolly," she pouted. "I've been reading about this ultra hot club in New York City called Studio 54. It's where all the crème de la crème hang out."

"Tina," I said in a calm non-judgmental voice. "I got two problems with that. First, fancy places like that spray for people like us. And second, Studio 54 closed sometime in the 80's."

"You've always got an excuse," she said, not troubling herself with logic. "We never go out."

"We went out last night."

"The Dairy Queen doesn't count." Her lips sagged into a frown and I could see I was genuinely making her feel lousy. I put on my best "sincere" face and switched into damage control.

"Baby, when I'm around you I'm on such a natural high it feels as if we're out on the town." I rubbed her wrist tenderly, sneaking glances to see if she was buying it. She wasn't, so I added: "I promise we'll go out more." She stared at me for a long beat, deliberating my fate, then finally spoke.

"Zolly, you're this close to losing me," she said, holding her hands in the air about four feet apart. We both laughed. "You're still my Zolly Bear." She giggled and tickled my chin with her finger.

This was not the time to remind her how much I hated being called her "Zolly Bear" so I just grinned and said "Yeah, I guess I am." Then our eyes met and I leaned in to kiss her. Tina was a great kisser whose lips could transport you to a new plane of existence, but after only a couple of seconds she suddenly pulled back, anger flashing across her face like wildfire.

"You've been eating zeppoles!" The accusation stunned me like a taser. I hunched back from the impact and my eyes widened like a deer caught in the headlights of a 747.

"Babe, no..." I stuttered.

"Don't lie to me Zolly. I can taste the oil on your lips and there's powdered sugar all over you!"

"Babe, I...I...." I sputtered, cornered like a rat with a powdered sugar moustache. Excuses flashed through my brain: A giant whale beached itself, plowed into the boardwalk, hit a zeppole stand, sent one flying into the air and against all odds it landed in my mouth. Nah, maybe not.

"This is how you plan to break it off, isn't it?" Tina whined sadly. "You don't have the guts to tell me it's over, so you'll just poison yourself with cholesterol till you kick off and leave me all alone!"

"I ain't kicking off anytime soon. I promise, Tina."

"Oh no?!" Her hand angrily flipped over a few more Tarot cards on the table top. "You see?!" she said, pointing to the smiling skull of the Grim Reaper. "Every time I deal your fortune this card comes up. It's creeping me out Zolly."

"Why the hell are you fooling around with this bullshit?"

"I was practicing. Your Aunt Margo says if I get good I can spell her on the boardwalk."

"Babe, don't you already have enough tending bar, doing all my secretary work and babysitting a thousand kids?"

"Zolly, I'm scared for you baby."

How could you not love this woman? I wrapped her in my arms and gave her a big hug. She's a good head taller than me, even in flats, and we must make a real comical sight together. But when Tina's in my arms, I don't care what it looks like. I only know how it feels. "You've got nothing to worry about sweetheart. I'll always be here," I promised from the bottom of my heart.

"Yeah?" she asked, not convinced. Then with a look of dread she pulled a waitress slip out of her apron pocket and placed it in my hand ruefully. I read it and gave her an excited smirk. "Sex on the Beach? It's a little kinky, but I'm game. I mean, as soon as it gets dark and the boardwalk closes."

"Ohhhh!" she squealed in frustration. "That's a drink order. Here." She turned the waitress slip over in my palm. There was a phone number scrawled across the back. "You got a call from Atlantic City. It's about that big deal murder, the singer's kid and all."

"Ariélle?! The Ariélle murder case?!" I whooped a bit too gleefully. "I knew it! When I was on the boardwalk I could smell it coming!" Seeing the look of dread on Tina's face I lowered my voice and became all business. "Interesting," I added flatly.

"Yeah, that Ariélle woman," Tina said. "I was never really a fan, were you?"

"Nah," I said, shaking my head. How could I tell her I was in love with Ariélle since I was fourteen and first saw one of her TV specials back in the 70's? How I took all my dough from mowing lawns and hopped a train to New York City to catch her concert at Radio City Music Hall.

There I sat in Radio City's cavernous barrel domed auditorium - a cave being the perfect setting for the primal transformation into manhood I was about to undergo. The house lights dimmed and it became pitch black. I felt like one of those fish that live so deep in the ocean they have never experienced sunlight. My eyes were useless, but my ears picked up the scraping, rustling sound of the Music Hall's giant curtain being parted. The stage remained totally dark, and then suddenly this narrow shaft of light came out of nowhere to illuminate a set of eyes.

Those eyes! They shimmered like two glowing ponds of liquid amber. They pierced the darkness like the eyes of a hungry tigress on the prowl, but at the same time betrayed a deep inner vulnerability - at once predator and prey.

"Ariélle."

That was her entire name. It was more than enough.

From that moment everything I knew about desire was tossed out the window – along with my Farah Fawcett poster. Suddenly all the girls in my school became drones in the beehive of love. Yeah I know that drones are males, but you never saw the girls in my school.

I bought all of Ariélle's albums and caught any B movie she even walked through. My walls were scotch taped over with pictures of her statuesque body and scolding lips. I embarrassed myself buying all variety of fan magazines, hoping to learn any scrap of information I could about this enigma. And she was a true enigma. No one could claim they knew from what part of the globe she came. No one could declare her ethnicity with any certainty. Even her accent was a riddle. Just when you thought you had your finger on its origin, it slipped away like quicksilver, and once again left you totally baffled. Rumors were rampant. Was she French? An Egyptian princess? Or as legend had it did this goddess simply emerge one day from deep inside the rain forests of Brazil? There were even those devotees who claimed that she was an alien, that no woman born of this earth could approach her beauty.

"I've got a bad feeling about this Zolly," Tina warned, pushing the Grim Reaper card to within an inch of my cornea like some kind of Gothic eye test.

"Tina, baby, you know my business. It's the same old same old. Ninety percent is unglamorous leg work, asking questions and weeding out the bullshit. There's never any real danger or thrills like you see in the movies." I put on my best "life is such a bore" face, but to myself I was screaming "The Ariélle murder! Holy Crap! Jackpot!"

Oh yeah, did I mention I make my living as a private investigator?

CHAPTER TWO

"Ariélle, Ariélle, Ariélle," how many times had I cried out that name in the throes of passion as I held her exquisite body over me. The passion. The ecstasy. The inevitable pain when one of those sharp advertising cards would fall from the People Magazine I was holding over my head and make a slice across the bridge of my nose. Okay, I was fourteen and possessed. So what if our love nest consisted of a twin bed with a wagon wheel headboard and Star Wars sheets? I was sure a woman of Ariélle's sophistication could look beyond all that and see the real me – whoever the hell that might be. I was also sure that it was destiny for me and Ariélle to be together someday. And now the stars were aligning and it was about to happen! Yes, destiny did exist. God sat in his Heaven.

Holly crap Zolly, don't go off the deep end man, I reminded myself. This was business. Her kid had been charged with murder and Ariélle needed my help. But wasn't that fate? I always say when you start down a road you never know where it's gonna lead you. Maybe this road would lead me someplace I had always dreamed about.

Tammara King, Ariélle's personal manager, filled me in on some of the details of the case over the phone, but didn't tell me much that wasn't already splashed over the front pages of all the newspapers. They all seemed to run the same photo of Ariélle leaving the courthouse in her now trademark "I want to be alone" look - dark glasses and a black scarf wrapped tightly around most of her head and face. "Singer's Kid Held on Murder Charge," "Murder She Sang!" "Like Mother, Like Daughter?" That last headline was from one of the more tabloidy of our distinguished newspapers and alluded to suspicions and rumors that Ariélle had been involved in the death of her husband Eric Von Strasbourg decades ago. Von Strasbourg was an entrepreneur. Funny, but whenever a rich famous woman is married to a guy who's basically a good looking bum, he's given the title "entrepreneur." But what the hell, chicks get horny too.

Like most bums, this Eric guy was never satisfied with his good fortune and spent a good deal of his time investing in foreign commodities – mainly German, Swiss, and Norwegian blondes. It all peaked with his well publicized affair with a Danish opera singer/porno star. At about the height of the press frenzy surrounding Von Strasbourg's cheating he was driving alone from a chalet in Colorado following a ski weekend with Ariélle and their young daughter. A snow storm intensified into a blizzard and Von Strasbourg's Porsche ran out of gas, stranding him in the middle of nowhere. By time rescuers found him he had frozen to death. I always thought it was appropriate he departed this life the way he lived it – stiff.

At the time there were all kinds of rumors about the wronged and humiliated Ariélle having reeked revenge on her philandering husband; but after the usual "celebrity light" investigation the pin prick found in the Porsche's fuel line was attributed to natural causes. But hey, everybody in Hollywood is issued one "Get out of a murder free" card. It comes in the gift basket with teeth whitener and Botox.

Now all these years later Ariélle's daughter, Sophia, was facing similar accusations. Sophia, or "Sissy," as she was most always called, was engaged to one Kyle Broder, a trainer at one of the local gyms in Atlantic City where Ariélle performed twelve weeks a year. "Trainer" is an occupation right up there with "entrepreneur." Her mother must have loved that.

A few days earlier a dazed Sissy had strolled into an Atlantic City police station, and over a café latte to calm her nerves calmly told the cops where they could find the body of the fiancée she had pumped full of bullets. The police checked out Sissy's hotel room at the Babylon Dynasty Casino Resort and sure enough they found the bullet riddled body of Kyle Broder.

When Sissy was charged with first degree murder people began to suspect that there might be something to this "like mother, like daughter" thing. But unlike the rumors about Ariélle having offed her husband there was a big difference here. And it was a difference that would make my job a million times harder. Sissy had signed a confession.

"Marone," I muttered as I thought about Sissy's confession and swung my car into the parking lot of the magnificent "Babylon Dynasty Casino Resort." For those of you who don't know any Italians "Marone" means something like "son of a bitch."

Feeling a sudden gnawing in my gut I popped a couple Maalox and stared out my window as the splendor of ancient Babylon spread out before me. I'm sure this is exactly how ancient Babylon would have looked if it was a twenty story high rise clad in smoked glass and had a giant electronic billboard advertising ninety-nine cent prime rib.

As I chewed my antacids I threaded my car through a legion of palace servants in gold headdresses and purple tunics parking cars, hailing cabs and toting luggage. Each and every one of them sported authentic Mesopotamian garb and genuine Jersey/Puerto Rican accents. Can you imagine how screwed the archeologists are gonna be when they dig this place up a couple thousand years from now?

Handing my keys to the valet I asked him to find a safe place for my baby. My Mini Cooper was my baby. I changed her oil regularly, bathed her, and wrapped her in swaddling chamois. I shampooed and groomed her upholstery and carpets so that they smelled as fresh as an alpine spring meadow. I treated her dash and tires with the latest chemical formulas, and waxed and buffed her exterior to protect her blushing red finish from the Jersey winters and pollution. I brought her into the dealer for check-ups more often than I saw my own doctor.

The valet responded with a contemptuous sigh that said "you call *this* a car?" Can you believe it? A superior put-upon sigh from a guy dressed in nothing but a gold loin cloth? Don't you just hate it when jerks working for minimum wage look down their nose at you? Yeah right buddy, you can condescend to me when you own the damn hotel, for now put in your forty hours and go home to your one bedroom apartment next to the Muffler shop. But don't get me started.

Already suffering post-partum syndrome I watched the valet drive my baby past a row of Mercedes, Jags, and Bentleys positioned strategically to announce the taste, wealth, and sophistication of the Babylon Dynasty's clientele. I knew my Mini Cooper would be strategically parked somewhere near Delaware.

What the hell. I adjusted the tilt of my fedora and set off for the Kingdom of Babylon.

Inside the lobby a Haitian dressed like Hammurabi directed me to the elevators. "Yo Mon, you passes 'round the Tower of Babel Bingo, carries your good self across the River Euphrates pass the craps tables, and you'll be finding them very same elevators besides the Hanging Gardens Coffee Shop." I tipped my head in appreciation and he tilted his in return, the gilded plastic snake coiled around his head dipping precariously close to my nose.

In a few minutes I was knocking on the double doors to a penthouse suite on the twentieth floor. I was greeted by a brawny young man who had to be at least six four and had a chest you could play hand ball against. His rugged good looks were complimented by boyish blonde bangs and a charming Texas drawl. From his build he looked like he could have played linebacker for the Dallas Cowboys.

"Mista Michel-angelo?" he asked, extending his beefy hand.

"Zolly," I replied. We shook and his grip felt like it was gonna turn my hand bones into paste.

"Pleasure I'm sure ta meet ya, sir. I'm Marshall, Ariélle's hairdresser."

Hairdresser? Maybe this guy's fantasies about playing with the Dallas Cowboys were a little different than what I had imagined. But okay, who am I to judge? I've always felt that being gay is like playing for the NFL. You've got no say which team is going to draft you.

"Why don't ya'll come in and have a seat sir? Miss Ariélle's taking care of some last minute business before her show. Can I get ya a drink or something?" Marshall offered.

"No thanks" I said as I sank into a sofa so plush it swallowed me up like quicksand.

"I hope ya don't mind me askin', but you're of I-talian descent I'm guessin'?"

"Yeah, that's right," I said, grabbing the sofa arm and trying to lift my butt up.

"Yes Sir I could tell. You people all just have the best hair."

"Yeah, well thanks," I said, rocking my body back and forth to gain momentum for an escape. It didn't work and I started to fear what I'd do if a fire broke out.

"You know if ya ever have the time I would love to do somethin' with ya."

"What?" I asked, a little homophobic panic entering my voice.

"Somethin' with that great hair of yours. Maybe we could update it a bit. Bring it a few decades closer to the twenty-first century! Ha!" His eyes twinkled and he laughed like a cowhand telling a dirty joke around a campfire. I swear I expected him to slap his knee.

"I'll take that as a compliment," I said.

"Why that's how it's all meant of course," he said, moving toward a closed door. "I'll tell them all you're here." Marshall nodded and gave me a devilish wink I couldn't decipher. Was he just one of those over-friendly types or was he making a pass?! I never saw myself coming off as the GQ type, but maybe my fedora and sharp blue blazer made me appear a little too dapper in certain circles. Suddenly I could commiserate with every woman who's gotten the wolf whistle on the street. I felt like a piece of meat.

At this point I had sunk so far down in the sofa I started looking around for a straw to breathe through if I went completely under. What a suite. I'd never seen anything like this at the Holiday Inn. I was in an expansive sitting area with several sofas, tables and a grand piano. Through an archway I could spy a full kitchen, and sunk right into the floor before a wall of windows was a huge spa tub. Beyond that was a spiral staircase leading up to God knows where, probably Mount Olympus. It was all part of a celebrity shadow-world schlubs like me never get to see.

"Zolly!" Suddenly my name was booming off the walls and I flashed back to my days at Fort Dix and Drill Sergeant Kleinschmidt. My head snapped around and I saw an athletic looking woman in a business suit coming at me like a projectile. "Tammara King," she said, exploding at my side. "We spoke on the phone."

It was Ariélle's manager, a broad shouldered athletic looking woman with black hair, black glasses, and intense black eyes that nailed you to the wall. Despite being not at all unattractive, she was the kind of woman who upon entering a room made you wish you were wearing a cup. "Yeah, nice to meet you, I..." We shook hands and my recently healed bones were pulverized once again. What the hell was it with these people and their vise-like grips? "Ayeeeeee, I winced. "I... remember. Good to meet you." I took advantage of her hold and used her hand as an anchor to leverage myself out of the man-eating sofa.

"Can you be trusted Mr. Michelangelo? Ariélle is a very private person, and I promise I will do anything necessary to protect that privacy."

She had the look in her eyes of a rancher about to geld a bull and I got the feeling she *would* do anything necessary. Her loyalty was admirable, but I had to set things straight. "Yeah I understand and respect all that. But her daughter's been accused of murder. I'm going to have to be free to ask personal questions or I'm just wasting everybody's time."

"Of course. But I'm sure as a professional you'll see the importance of establishing some rules before I can grant you access to Ariélle."

Access? This wasn't exactly a meeting with the President or an audience with the Pope. But I'd seen Tammara King's kind a million times before. You give an overzealous nobody a little responsibility and they start to inflate their importance and take their job a little too seriously. It was a lot like the pimply fifteen year old kid at the movie theater who eyeballed your ticket to be sure you didn't cheat and buy a senior's admission. Not that I'd ever do anything like that. Despite them charging five hundred bucks for a box of Raisinettes.

"First rule – all contact with Ariélle has to come through me. I'll make sure to get anything important to her immediately, but don't want her bothered by trivia or disturbed by phone calls in the middle of the night."

Oh brother, I knew I'd have better luck getting in to see the Mighty Wizard of Oz than getting past this chick. As Tammara rattled on I smiled and pretended to listen while picturing in my head that she was a barking seal. When her jaw finally stopped flapping I threw her a fish by agreeing to the phone screening thing, all the time saying to myself "dream on, Sister." Unfortunately she wasn't done.

"And whatever you do, please do not bore Ariélle by asking things like how old she is or does she currently have a man in her life... and most especially don't ask about her accent or where she was born."

"That would be so bush league," I said, striking "what's that accent?" and "where were you born?" off my mental list.

"Thank you for understanding. This way." Tammara directed with an officious phony smile. She led me to the door I had seen Marshall disappear through and stepping inside I suddenly found myself in total darkness. I heard the door close behind me and it sent a shiver down my spine. Was it my imagination or was it a good ten degrees cooler in here? For a moment I was overcome by that creepy feeling I got as a kid the first time I walked into the haunted house on the amusement pier. I was hoping the outcome wouldn't be the same because I didn't have an extra pair of underpants with me this time either.

"Zahlee I need you." There it was. Out of the Heavens. That voice! The very definition of an enigma; it was at once smoke and honey, angel and siren, Madonna and dominatrix. Half spoken, half moaned, the breathy words were the same I had heard over and over in my head as a youth. "Zahlee, I need you." Only now they were real, spoken by a live woman. It was Ariélle! She was here in this very room!

At least I thought she was. It was so dark I couldn't see my nose in front of my face.

Suddenly there was the whirr of an electric motor and the remote controlled drapes parted enough to allow the scant remaining sunlight of the day into the room. "Better Zahlee?" she asked. Her tongue held onto my name as if giving it up grudgingly, and "better" sounded more like "butter." What *was* that accent that had a way of gliding over vowels and softening consonants? Was it French? No, not quite. It was a little like French but blended with something else. Cajun maybe? Or maybe it reflected the French influence on Polynesian?

Suddenly something stirred across the room and in the shadows I could see her now! Ariélle. As my eyes adjusted I could see she was wearing the skintight black cat suit in which she began every show. It clung to her lithe body as if she had been dipped in liquid dark chocolate. She sat motionless again, perched on a throne of pillows atop a long white divan. Her long legs thrust to a side and curled back under her, causing her body to form a sensuous "Z." I had to stare at her for several long moments before what my eyes were showing me could be absorbed by my brain.

But something was off, something was wrong. Her eyes! I couldn't see her eyes. They were hidden behind the dark glasses she had become famous for wearing in public. But the room was nearly pitch black. What was she expecting, a comet to shoot through and blind us?

"Zahlee?" she asked with a lilting, lonesome tone. I was at once touched by the vulnerability in her voice and puzzled once again as to the origin of her accent.

"I'm here, Ma'am," I finally answered. "It's truly a pleasure to meet you."

"Come sit." She pointed to an ottoman before her and I obeyed like a lap dog. My knees were now within inches of touching Ariélle's knees! Okay, maybe within feet. It was like saying you were close to wrestling a lion, had the zoo not built a moat between you. "I assume zee pit bull has filled you in?" she asked.

"The wha-?" I stammered.

"Zee 'pit bull.' That's zee endearing name we all hahve for my manager Miss King, because when she sinks her teeth into somezing she does not let go. I am fortunate to have someone as loyal as Tammara watching over me. Did you know she was a soldier during zee first Gulf War? She iz not a perzan to cross."

That was an understatement. After doing some homework I picked up a bunch of interesting stories about this Tammara King. Despite having an excellent military record and commendations up the wazoo, she was once reprimanded for commandeering an M1 Abrams battle tank off her base in Georgia. Apparently she drove it down Main Street to the front door of a used car dealership that refused to take back a lemon they'd sold her cousin.

"I wasn't planning to cross anyone," I said, turning back to Ariélle with a big grin. "But thanks for the warning."

"I believe you," she said, placing her long delicate fingers over her heart. "I learned a long time ago zhat if you need zee truth about somezing in this town you ask zee pit bosses. And zee pit bosses tell me you are zee best investigator on zee East Coast."

"That's very flattering, thank you, Ma'am." My eyes couldn't help but be drawn to the milky white fingers resting against her breast. Oh to be a finger.

"Zahlee, do not let zem take my daughter from me."

"I swear I'll do my best, Ma'am. The only thing is, well, it's gonna be tough with her making a confession and all."

"I know in my heart zhat Sissy isn't capable of killing anyone. My attorneys will change her plea once I get her to come to her zenses."

"Do you have any idea why Sissy would confess to such a thing?"

"Zee man she was to marry is dead. She's confused and in shock. And..." Her voice trailed off.

"And?"

"All her life Sissy and I have been more like sisters zhan mother and daughter. We tell each other everyzing. But these past few months I've felt her pulling away, becoming distant. I've sensed that she has a very large secret she's trying to keep from me. Find zhat secret Zahlee."

The secret, yeah there's always a secret. It's what keeps me employed. It's why I get up in the morning – other than the pancakes.

"If Sissy's trying to hide something I'll get to the bottom of it," I assured Ariélle. "But I have to speak frankly here if I may."

"If you're not honest with me zen what is our purpose?"

"Good. So let me just say this. Sometimes after an entire lifetime with someone we think we know them. Then something happens to that person. It puts them in a situation that causes them to do something even they didn't think they were capable of."

"Sissy did not kill him," Ariélle said as if reading the words off a stone tablet.

"So she and her fiancée, this Kyle, things were good between them?"

"Yes. Sissy was happier zhan I hahve ever seen her. It was like a burden had been lifted off her shoulders."

"A burden?"

"Zee stories of my daughter's wild life are well documented. I can't tell you how many times I have searched my soul to try and understand where I've failed her."

Jesus being a parent isn't easy. There are times when I see an adorable little infant crawling across the floor, smiling and goo-gooing, that I feel real bad not having kids. Then I'll hear about some kid stabbing their old man to death for drug money and a big grin spreads over my face.

"At first I thought Sissy was zust showing zee rebellious streak she'd inherited from me. It was almost fun sharing zee reckless defiance to doing what zee world expected. But zen when her behavior started to become self-destructive I decided, perhaps too late, zhat she didn't need a friend, but a mother. So I cut her allowance back and put all her money in a trust she couldn't touch until she settled down."

"Tough love. Did it help?"

"At first I thought it did. Sissy met and fell in love with zis soccer player – I know, a sweaty man who makes hiz living kicking a ball with hiz foot. But he seemed devoted to her and for a time I thought Sissy had finally found her true love. They got engaged and quickly married. But zen after a little while it didn't seem to be enough for Sissy. It was almost as if she seemed to be happier for me than for herself zhat she had settled down. Zee restlessness came back. It was if she was still searching for something. 'The father she never knew' was zee answer zee psychiatrists gave me, about a hundred thousand dollars later."

I whistled. For a hundred grand she could have hired an actor to play her dad and take the kid for a pony ride once and awhile. Wow. What ever happened to making a kid sit in the corner? Even if it didn't work it was a hell of a lot cheaper.

"She left zee soccer player and from zere found a succession of other men she 'settled' on; each one worse zan zee last. And zen, zen zere was J-Up."

J-Up? She dated a soft drink? "Who?" I asked.

"Jamie Upton. From zhat dreadful boy band *Downtown Dudes*. Lord if she didn't have taste for men she should hahve at least had better taste in music! How could she be my daughter? If I hadn't carried her in my womb I'd have insisted on a DNA test."

"J-Up. Oh yeah, I've heard of him." Or I thought I did. All I could picture was one of those androgynous boys pre-teen girls scream over at concerts. The kind with the cutesy innocent looks and brooding salacious leers. For girls making the transition to womanhood they offered a safe fantasy - something analogous to having sex with your Teddy Bear. The problem for J-Up and his kind was that the pre-teen girls soon move on to the next flavor-of-the-month hormone magnet.

His band history, and his talent limited to his ability to thrust his hips, J-Up attempted to extend his fifteen minutes of fame by crossing over into the world of rap music. The only problem was the public demanded he cross over to oblivion.

"J-up was zee worst. I blame him for any real problems Sissy had with drugs," Ariélle said. "Before him sure zere was drinking and whatever goes on with zee partying, but he was serious trouble."

"If I remember right she was supposed to marry him too wasn't she?" Ariélle laughed. "Marry? I don't even know what zhat word means anymore. Does it mean two people who are sinking to zee bottom of a lake desperately grabbing onto each other before zey reach bottom? If so zen maybe you could call it a marriage."

"Luckily she changed her mind," I said as the memory of their very public breakup came back to me. J-Up had made a royal stink about being dumped. You couldn't turn on an entertainment magazine show without seeing clips of J-Up crying about how much he loved Sissy and wanted her back. Then in the next breath he'd be shouting like a schizoid about how she'd wronged him, and how he wasn't going to let her get away with it.

"It was a miracle. I don't know if Sissy got tired of his neediness, or if she was still searching for what eluded her, but she finally cut him loose."

Ariélle continued. "And zhat made all the difference. Zee drugs stopped. Zee partying stopped. She showed little interest in even dating. It was as if she realized she had sunk to zee bottom of zee lake and the weight of zee water was crushing her. She needed to get to zee surface and breathe again."

I looked at Ariélle and suddenly saw the poet that was evident in all her songs. Being a poet and romantic myself I wanted to leap across the space between us and land on top of her. I just couldn't think of a word to rhyme with "police."

"Zis is when she met Kyle," Ariélle went on, oblivious to the evil thoughts in my head. It's a good thing women can't read minds or they'd never leave the house. "For zee first time

Sissy seemed truly happy. She had found whatever it was she was searching for so long."

"It doesn't make sense Ma'am. I mean, why if she had finally found her true love would Sissy... why would she destroy it?"

"She couldn't have."

"But she confessed to it."

"I am sure she is not telling zee whole truth, zhat she's protecting someone. And my instincts tell me zee place to begin is J-Up."

"Hmmm, you may be right."

"Promise you won't let zem take Sissy from me. Promise me Zahlee."

"I swear I'll do everything possible to prevent it, Ma'am." My promise seemed to calm her. She became quiet, almost as if meditating. When she spoke she was no longer the concerned mother, but the enigmatic seductress once again.

"Do not call me 'Ma'am.' My name is Ariélle," she said breathlessly. And with that she removed her dark glasses and revealed the eyes that long ago possessed my soul. "Save my child, Zahlee. I will be eternally grateful."

She owned me once again.

CHAPTER THREE

I always like to get as much information as I can about a
case before talking to the accused. It improves my "bullshit
detector." So the next day I visited the cop house in Atlantic
City. I had to circle the block a few times to find a safe place
to park my baby. It was summer and you had to avoid trees
that could drip sap onto the finish or shed leaves that would
burry themselves in the windshield wiper well. I hated that.
You never could get them all out, they seemed to breed in
there like some alien virus.

As I stood on the steps of the station I stared up at the
prehistoric red brick facade and felt a pinch in my throat.
There were a lot of memories here. This was my home for
many years. I thought it always would be – until that day I
dropped my badge and gun on the desk and walked out. But
no need to drag all that up now.

I pushed inside the double mahogany doors and found
myself in a long coffin shaped room almost two stories
high. The sounds of keyboards, police radios and human
conversation echoed off the tin ceiling. No expense was
spared to create a delightful work place. The walls floor and

ceiling were decorated in every color of the rainbow – as long as the rainbow was a moldy green. Paint peeled off the window frames and mixed with a layer of dust on the sills. The air was close and had that unmistakable institutional smell of a bank or school. Wafting through was a definite hint of old gym shorts.

I made my way unnoticed past the eagle eye of the desk sergeant perched high atop the floor on a raised platform. So much for Homeland Security. Walking to the back I found the detective pool, a bunch of gray metal desks and file cabinets organized in a haphazard pattern untouched by human logic.

There he was in all the magnificence of his Creator! A gelatinous mass of two-hundred and fifty pounds, located mostly in his belly, hunched over a desk, his keen mind searching for the latest forensic break-through in the morning's Racing Form. He wore the one sport coat he owned – fashioned from a sort of tweed/asphalt material whose indestructible properties even Superman would envy. Suddenly one of his thick gray brillo-like eyebrows arched up as he found something of interest. Blindly his hand stabbed for a pencil and knocked over his paper coffee cup. The tan liquid flooded Moses style over the edge of his desk onto a pair of pants molecularly more coffee bean than rayon.

My former partner in all his glory.

"Slowicki!" I called sharply as I approached. His real name was "Sowicki," but I changed it to "Slow" to befit his sloth-like manner. It stuck so good no one used his real name anymore. "Hey, Slowicki, there's a new invention, it's called 'standing up.'"

His bloodshot eyes turned on me like a bull in the slaughterhouse. "Then why don't *you* stand up?" he shot back. It sounded like a dump truck unloading a load of gravel. "Oh, sorry, you already are!" His belly heaved in a laugh that threatened the buttons on his threadbare white shirt.

Then in a deft move at once insulting to me and begging for a sexual harassment suit, he turned to a female officer bending over a file cabinet. "Hey girlie, did you hear Zolly's using a new sexual aide? It's called a 'ladder.'" He heaved again and a brave button took one for the team. "I got a million of 'em!"

"Too bad they ain't brain cells," I said dryly as I took a seat in front of his desk. "What have you got on the Sissy Von Strasbourg case?"

"Ariélle's kid?" Slowicki's lips curled into a surprised arch. "Who the hell did you have to promise *not* to sleep with to get a case like that?"

"Cut to the chase and there's the usual in it for you," I said with impatience. Slowicki took the bribe and attempted to lift himself out of his chair. This was no easy task considering his bulk and the fact the chair was on rollers. It slid back and forth several times as Slowicki's hands gripped the desk and his body teetered. The spectacle was worthy of a pay-per-view event. Finally making it to his feet the detective lumbered over to a bank of dented file cabinets. After an eternity he returned, wheezing, and carrying a manila folder so old and wrinkled it originally held an all points bulletin for John Wilkes Booth.

"Let's see," Slowicki grumbled in his sandblasted voice as he browsed the report. It was like talking to a frog. "Victim Kyle Broder... scene of the crime... Room 652 of the Babylon Dynasty."

"Any witnesses?"

Slowicki squinted at the report. He still needed to slide his finger down the page to read. "Hummm ackkkk" he hacked. "Let's see ... witnesses...."

Turns out the murder took place on a Monday morning, the slowest day of the week for Atlantic City. A hell of a lot of their business is people coming down on day trips. Most people staying over and needing a hotel room hit the place on the weekends and are gone by Monday morning. And any big conventions haven't usually checked in that early. So only a handful of rooms on the sixth floor where the murder took place were even rented. And of those there were only a few whose occupants weren't down in the casino, coffee shop, or out on the town.

The first witness was a middle aged insurance salesman from Evansville Indiana staying in a room a few doors down. He heard gunshots but thought they were coming from a TV. He'd called the front desk the night before to complain about the asshole in the room next to him leaving the TV on loud even when he was out of the room. When pressed to give a time he heard the shots he said they were sometime before Eleven A.M. when he stepped into the shower.

The best witnesses were a young couple from Philadelphia on their honeymoon. They were able to pinpoint the time of the shots to exactly eight minutes before Eleven. They'd been awakened out of a sound sleep by the shots and the groom remembers glancing over at the alarm clock on the night table. When asked why he hadn't reported the shots the groom said he thought they were probably fireworks. And if they weren't it wasn't exactly something he wanted stick his nose in. Ah the wellspring of human compassion. You could fill a good sized wading pool. But don't get me started.

I asked Slowicki if there were any other witnesses. It took a couple of minutes for my question to make its way through the calcified nerve endings between his ear and his brain. But he finally answered. "Nobody else... they questioned a maid working the floor but she didn't see nothing."

I jotted down the names and info on the witnesses, then asked "What about the weapon?"

"Uhh, a .38 special." He read on, mouthing the words and clicking his tongue. "Hah! This was no accident, the chickie emptied the gun. And bingo! She signed a confession. My heartfelt condolences Zolly."

"Yeah, I'm sure...You recover all the slugs?"

"Six" he said absentmindedly, still engrossed in the report. "Lookie here."

"What?"

"The .38's registered to her momma, that Ariélle dame. Man would I love to get in her..."

"Prints?! What about prints?" I demanded, unable to bear the image of Slowicki getting anything into anybody, let alone my beloved Ariélle.

Slowicki made a grunt that sounded something like "hudd." His head slumped forward and he seemed to stop breathing. For a moment I thought a French fry had finally blocked his last functioning artery.

"Hello? Dammit Slowicki, move a little so we know whether to call the undertaker."

"Funny thing," he answered from somewhere in oblivion. "There were no prints on the gun. She must have wiped them clean... I guess this Sissy isn't as big a dope as everybody says."

I slumped back in my chair and stared at the little plastic palm tree on Slowicki's desk. It was the kind with the green plastic fronds and was in the middle of a plastic dish where you keep a turtle. The turtle either died or was eaten by Slowicki decades ago, but he kept the palm tree as a reminder. His dream was to get out of the cold Jersey winters and retire to Florida with his wife. Well, that wasn't going to happen.

As I mulled over the evidence the fact that there were no prints on the gun was something to pin hope on. I got an idea. "What about the tests for gunpowder residue on Sissy's hands?" I asked matter-of-factly, mentally crossing my fingers. Slowicki got lost in the report again, flipping back and forth between the pages with a confused look on his face. Of course he always wore a confused look similar to a cat watching a lava lamp, so it didn't mean much.

Finally he set the report down and mumbled "There ain't any."

"What?" I said, acting surprised but hoping all the time there wouldn't be. "No one tested her for powder?"

"For Christ's sake Zolly," Slowicki muttered defensively. "She waltzed in here and confessed to killing her boyfriend. And everything at the scene checked out like she said."

"Yeah, well sometimes what people say isn't always true, like half the guys around here who call themselves 'detectives.'" I regretted saying that as soon as the words came out of my mouth. I was being too hard on Slowicki. He was one of the good guys and this wasn't even his case. "C'mon," I said. "Let's hit Clemente's. I'm hungry." Slowicki took that as a peace offering and miraculously was able to almost spring out of his chair.

As we walked out of the station house I was feeling a little more positive about the case. At least there were no eye-witnesses, no prints, and we'd never know if Sissy had residue from firing the gun on her hands. It was going to be hard as hell to overcome a confession, but at least if no one saw what happened there was no one to contradict Sissy's version of the truth. Maybe we could get her to change her story, or failing that, maybe get her to cop to something less than Murder in the First degree. I was looking for any hairline crack I could drive a chisel in.

Forty minutes later I was standing in the morgue with Detective Slowicki and Chief Coroner Slowicki. Did I mention he was half of a set of twins? I didn't want to scare you. Identical Slowickis. The only way to tell them apart was the detective had gout in his right foot, the coroner in his left. Believe me, you wouldn't want to look that close to find that out, but details are an important part of my business.

On the table in front of me lay the pale gray corpse of Kyle Broder - literally a poor stiff. Like I say, when you start down a road you never know where it's gonna lead you. Here he was getting all ready for his wedding day, and surprise, his bride-to-be was already calculating the exact date of "Till death do us part." A real shame. No matter how many corpses you see you never get used to the finality of death. After a life of ups and downs, hopes and dreams, loves and losses, you're left with nothing but a rack of meat.

Speaking of which, on a side table the twins were tearing into a bag of bribe money like jackals into the corpse of a Butterball antelope. Well, okay, to be fair there wasn't any money in the bag; just two meatball and mozzarella heroes from Clemente's Sub Hut.

"So Doc," I said, interrupting the feeding frenzy. "Could you put down the sandwich and tell me what we've got here?" I was losing patience. Don't get me wrong, I love food as much as the next guy, okay, more; but there's a time and a place for everything. Food is like a woman, you have to take your time with it, savor it. The Slowickis were dishonoring the sandwich.

The Coroner said "Wahh goat teee blet wooms," or something like that. It was hard to hear through the meatball stuffing his mouth like a mute in a trumpet. I waited until he swallowed and then quickly before he could take another bite jumped in.

"What?"

"We got three bullet wounds."

"Three wounds, you're sure? Because the police report says six rounds were fired."

"But only three hit the guy," Detective Slowicki chimed in, wiping a glob of tomato sauce off his chin. "They found slugs sprayed all over the room. All six." He punctuated his sentence with a chomp worthy of a T-Rex.

"That's right," Chief Coroner Slowicki confirmed. "Three bullet wounds." He proceeded to show off the entry wounds using the end of his sub as a pointer. "One strikes the forearm and nicks the ulna before passing through... A second barely grazes the fleshy part of the thigh... but this, this baby is what does the poor bastard in. Bang!" he shouted as his hand holding the sub recoiled like a fired pistol.

"Three," I said, chewing it over mentally and looking at a hole right through the victim's heart.

"Yeah, they weren't fooling around with this one," Coroner Slowicki said. He went on to explain how the first two wounds were inflicted from a distance, but the final fatal shot was fired at close range. "They weren't taking any chances."

Clucking my tongue sadly I moved in for a closer look and was shocked by what I discovered. "Holy crap! Is that fresh blood?!" The Coroner looked puzzled and followed my horrified stare to the victim's chest. He reached down to the squiggle of crimson, gathered it on his finger, and raised it to his eye for inspection. The in a move that almost caused me to lose my breakfast he stuck the finger in his mouth and tasted it!

"Uhhhhhhhhh gaahh noooooooo!" I groaned, doubling over and grabbing my stomach. The Coroner looked at me, cold and detached.

"Marinara," he said with a glint in his eye.

CHAPTER FOUR

Other than being Ariélle's daughter Sissy had two claims to fame. The first was being the unofficial Guinness Book of World Records designee as the planet's stupidest person. Once on a late night talk show Sissy was asked what she thought about global warming. She said she didn't mind it because she looked awesome in a bikini. On another occasion while appearing on a quiz show called something like "Are You Smarter Than a Sea Slug?" she located Pakistan on a map just below Illinois. There is, however, no documented evidence that Sissy once stated her belief that Mount Rushmore was a natural phenomenon.

Sissy's second claim to fame was being what they today call "a bad girl." In the past we would have chosen our words more carefully and simply called her a "whore." So many men came and went from her bedroom she had a machine that issued numbers like a deli counter. In response to her mother's frequent demands for Sissy to settle down, she'd been married or engaged at one time or another to a professional soccer player, the singer in a boy band, a Saudi mime, her auto mechanic, and a minister she'd been referred to for counseling.

To be fair Sissy's promiscuity had deep seated roots in her well chronicled abuse of drugs and alcohol. One of the highlights of this chronicle was her appearance on You Tube frolicking nude in the waters at Lourdes. Someone had told her the curative waters could prevent cellulite. Also available for download was the infamous sex tape made by her soccer player boyfriend that lead to her affectionately being given the nickname "Score!" But whatever you think of her morals, Sissy had never been in any real trouble before the murder charge. The closest she'd come was an arrest for driving on the wrong side of the San Diego Freeway at four in the morning. To be fair once again, we can't be sure if she was under the influence or merely too dumb to read the words "Wrong Way."

Sometime the next morning Ariélle's team of high-priced lawyers darkened the sky as they descended on Atlantic City like Pterodactyls. Despite Sissy's signed confession, they pled her "not guilty" at the arraignment and by late afternoon she was out on bail. Ain't justice grand? And being filthy rich don't hurt either.

I gave Sissy some time to collect herself before questioning her and she wisely chose to spend it doing an interview for *Entertainment Tonight.* When I finally found myself outside the Babylon the sun was beginning to set over the Atlantic and the beach was empty except for a couple guys with metal detectors. I didn't realize it at the time but they had a lot better chance of finding something than I did.

As the elevator reached Sissy's floor I could hear a commotion in the hall even before the doors opened. When I stepped out I saw two King Kongs in private security uniforms book ending a runt of a young man. Each guard held the kid up by a scrawny arm and had him literally suspended in air. His feet paddled the empty space above the carpet and his body twisted, rose and dipped as if performing some manic routine on the parallel bars. All the time he was struggling to shout over his shoulder toward an open door down the hall. The runt's face sported what might have once been a fashionable two-day growth, but the beard was unkempt and had developed into a six-day jungle. He wore tight black leather pants, a black leather vest over a tan, wrinkled suede shirt, and a black leather beret. Horses were giving up their lives all over the country to make up this kid's wardrobe.

"You're gonna be sorry girl! You're gonna miss J-Up. You're gonna want me so bad it's gonna hurt. It's gonna hurt like... like... pain! Bad pain!" the runt ranted. He was answered by the slam of the door his tirade was aimed at. "Don't you slam that door on me you f-ing bitch!" he screamed. Then in the next schizophrenic instant his voice became tender and plaintive. "Ah c'mon, baby, you know I love you. What do I have to do to prove it baby?! I need you. I need you so much.

What do I have to do?!" Then turning on a dime he became nasty again. "F-ing bitch! You'll get yours!"

Overtaken by melancholy he dropped his chin onto his chest and began to sob. The guards dragged him past me to the elevator. As the doors opened and their chunky bodies stepped in you could see the floor bounce like a butcher's scale. I looked into the elevator at the sobbing kid and he must of sensed it because he lifted his head up and his red eyes made contact with my own. "Life sucks, dude. It really sucks," he muttered.

"Amen," I said, giving him a nod and a tip of my hat. Either my answer, or the realization that he was talking to a stranger seemed to agitate him again. He jutted his chin out and growled.

"Get lost, man, I don't do the f-ing autograph thing."

"I wasn't going to give you one," I chuckled as the elevator doors closed. Then I took out my notepad to check Sissy's room number. When I reached it I discovered it was the very room I had seen the celebrity runt being dragged from.

I knocked on the door and was met once again by Marshall the cowboy hairdresser. "Ev'ning, Mr. Z." He was grinning like someone out of the cast of *Oklahoma*. I expected a chorus line in chaps to come dancing out of the closet. Poor choice of words, sorry.

"Damn, what's with these women?" I asked. "Are you a 24 hour live-in hairdresser?"

"Just part of the family," he answered proudly.

"No offense, but these people look for ways to throw money away. You don't see me traveling around with my barber."

"All ya have to do is look at your hair to prove that, sir. Do ya'll have a pet parrot or is that a cowlick?" The room cracked with the thunder of his loud chuck wagon laugh. He wet his hand and smoothed down a rarely errant patch of hair on the back of my head. "Not sure if that helps or not," he said with another laugh as he moved toward the bathroom and knocked on the door. "Sissy, the fashionista police have arrived."

He was answered by a frustrated female scream from behind the door. "Ohhhhh! Does it ever end?! I'll be out in a minute."

"Say listen, Marshall. That kid I saw the guards dragging down the carpet, did he come out of this room?"

"Oh yeah," Marshall nodded as he packed his hairdressing stuff into a leather bag. Leather again. Definitely a bad time to be a cow.

"Was he that, uh, what's his name? That Seven-up guy?"

Marshall let loose a horse laugh.

"Damned if ya ain't amusing Mr. Z. Have you listened to the radio since Abba broke up?"

"Shit! They broke up?!" I said with alarm. Marshall stared at me in shock and it was my time to laugh. "Heh! I'm just putting you on, partner."

"Good one!" His head tilted back and he whinnied again.

"But the kid, that was Jamie, J-Up or whatever the hell he calls himself?"

"Sure was." But it ain't no big deal. Sissy has a restraining order and once a week or so J-Up tests it to prove he still loves her."

"Sounds like he's still got it bad."

"I guess. A lot depends on whether there are TV cameras around. Listen, I wouldn't mention his name around Sissy, she's having one of her days."

"What kind of day?"

"The Monday, Tuesday, Wednesday, Thursday, Friday, Saturday, Sunday kind," he said with a wink.

"Oh that will be helpful, thanks for the tip."

Marshall opened door to the hall and on his way out smiled back at me. "Good luck with 'Tits on a Stick."

What the hell did he mean by that? "J-Up," "Tit's on a Stick," Didn't anybody name their kid "Fred" anymore?

It didn't take me long to find out what Marshall meant because almost immediately Sissy Strasbourg came bursting through the bathroom door.

"Zolly! Thank God you're here!" she shrieked, flailing her arms in the air dramatically. This was the skinniest woman I had ever laid eyes on. I guess it's true the camera adds ten pounds because in every picture I'd ever seen of Sissy she looked skinny, yeah, but the chick in front of me was so thin I was afraid if I touched her I'd get a paper cut. I swear she could have climbed into her blue jeans through a leg hole.

Everything about her was skinny except for a huge set of store bought breasts that made her so top heavy it seemed to put her in danger of teetering over at any moment. She wore five-hundred dollar dungarees and one of those bullshit socially conscious tees that said "End hunger." Only the words "End Hunger" were spelled out in hand beading that cost enough to feed a third world village for a month. Gazing at her stilt-like body and the large breasts bulging through "hunger," I understood why behind her back people called her "Tits on a Stick."

"Zolly, I desperately need your help," Sissy pleaded. Her voice had that elitist taint of the spoiled Beverly Hills brat, but somehow she had avoided picking up her mother's accent, whatever the heck accent that was.

"I understand how traumatic this all is. I promise I'll do everything I can to help," I said in my most reassuring voice. She gave me a confused look, cocking her head like a mutt hearing a silent whistle, then picked up a newspaper and shoved it in my face.

"This picture of me at the arraignment is in every paper! Oh God, what a nightmare! Tell me honestly Zolly, my life depends on it ... do you think I look fat?"

"Wha?" I said, stunned as if my head had just been clapped inside a giant bell.

"That hideous jailhouse jumpsuit. Orange was never my color. Do you think I look fat?"

Whoa, I'm smart enough to know better than answer a woman when she asks "do I look fat?" So I gave her my safe stock answer: "You look perfect."

"Perfect?!" she asked with alarm. "Perfect as in unnatural, like I've had too much work done? Not that I have... any, had any work done."

"Look sweetheart, I'm sure if Solomon were in the room he could figure out an answer to that. But would you mind if we sat down and discussed your possible murder sentence?"

"If we have to," she said with a pout.

"You don't think we should?"

"It won't make a difference Zolly. I'm only talking to you to make Mommy happy. I did what I did and nothing can change that. I just want this whole thing to be over!"

Jeez Marie. "Look Miss, I just need to ask a few questions so I can be straight in my own head about what went down. I want to make sure we're not missing something important. I know it will make your mother rest easier."

"Okay. I want to make this the least horrible I can for Mommy. Why don't we sit?"

"Good." We took seats across from each other in a sofa and armchair. "Now try and relax. I'm here to help you. Talk to me like a friend."

"Okay. I'll try. I mean most of my friends are women, and most of the guys in my life are... well, a different 'type' but I'll try."

Despite Marshal's warning I jumped right in and tossed a grenade. "That was quite a ruckus in the hall a minute ago. I walked right into it getting off the elevator."

Sissy gave me a put-upon roll of her eyes, sighed in frustration and then stared blankly. After thirty seconds I began to wonder if she understood that a conversation meant I'd say something and then it would be her turn to talk. I trudged on as if crossing a swamp in lead boots.

"So this Jamie character, this J-Up, what's up with the guy?"

She sighed again. "He thinks he's in love with me."

"And do you love him?"

"No... Well maybe once I thought I did, but not anymore."

"But you were engaged to him?"

"It was the dumbest thing I ever did." The dumbest? What a competition that must have been. "But I'm a different person now."

Oh brother, I'd be careful about creating another "me." There was precious little brain matter to go around. To my surprise Sissy continued without me having to shoot off a flare. "Jamie was part of my old life. I was kind of out of control back then. You may have heard about it."

Heard about it? If you googled the word "sex" more than half the entries would include photos of Sissy. But I was kind and simply nodded. "Yeah."

"Well, I've moved on with my life, and I guess J-Up hasn't. But he's harmless." She sighed wearily, becoming the martyr now.

"Oh? Harmless? Is that why you got a restraining order against him?"

"He's more an annoyance than a danger. Especially in shoe stores. He had it in his mind that I'd come to my senses and be his girl again. So I guess my engagement to Kyle was really hard on him. He swore if he couldn't have me nobody could."

"That sounds like a threat to me."

"Oh, it's all just part of his image. He thinks he's this big tough gangsta rapper now. He likes to make people think he's from the projects."

In fact I'd learn from research later that J-Up, a.k.a. Jamie Upton, was born in a Kansas suburb to a Presbyterian minister and a mother famous for her crocheted poodles. The kid couldn't have been any more white bread if he were born in a Wonder Bread factory.

"Good. This is all good to know, every little thing helps no matter how unimportant it seems. You're doing good."

"Thanks. I think it's because of my training as an actress, you know?"

No, I didn't know. In fact I had no clue what she meant, but I pressed on. "Now I know it's painful, but I need you to tell me about your fiancée Kyle."

"Okay... Um, we were engaged."

"Yeah, that's usually what the word 'fiancée' implies... Tell me how you met."

"Mommy works at the Babylon a lot and it's like our second home. Actually our second home is in Barbados, no maybe that would be our place in Vail. Anyway, I'm here a lot and I've made a lot of friends."

"So you met Kyle through a friend?"

"No. I hired him as a trainer."

"I see." My head shook like a tuning fork. I waited several moments for her to continue before finally having to prompt her. "And... eventually you two fell in love."

"We were engaged." I was beginning to feel like I was watching *Sesame Street* and the word for today was "engaged."

"Okay, you were engaged. We've established that. Why don't you try telling me what happened that night, the night Kyle died?"

"The night I shot him?" she asked. Holy crap, she might just as well have tied a red ribbon around her neck and given herself to the prosecutor as a Christmas present.

"Let's not try to make assumptions and draw conclusions, that's the D.A.'s job, okay?"

"But I killed him!"

"There. That's a perfect example of what I'm talking about. I'm thinking the less you blurt out 'I killed him!' the better your chances of getting off." I wiped my brow with a hankie. This was harder work than the coal mining my grandfather gave his life to, and I was beginning to sweat like a suckling pig at a Weight Watchers meeting. "Okay, look. Tell me what happened that night. Where were you? What were you doing?"

"Um. I was in my room here at the hotel. Not this room, it was all bloody and messy there, so they moved me."

My jaw dropped in disbelief. "Go on please."

"I was in my room, waiting for Kyle. He came over and we had this big fight and I shot him."

"Jeeeeeeezzzzzzzz!" I shouted, my whole body twisting in frustration. The 'I shot him' again! I wanted to shoot her and put us both out of our misery, but instead I bit my tongue and forced myself to calm down. "What was the fight about?"

"Um. It was a couple's thing. Does it really matter?"

"To some people, like a jury, it might yeah." This chick was so dumb if you gave her dirt and water she couldn't figure out how to make mud.

"Well, I suppose it was because Kyle wanted to break off the engagement."

"He did? Why?"

"He didn't say."

"Oh, I see, he didn't say. It happens," I said. But I was thinking that maybe the poor SOB broke it off because he learned you were dumber than a saw horse!

I took a deep breath. I was a professional. I had a job to do. "Can you tell me what happened next?"

"The argument got out of control. I was getting so angry I couldn't think!" I won't even make a crack about that remark, it's too easy. "I looked around the room. I saw the nightstand. I opened the drawer and took out the gun Mommy gave me for protection... and I shot him."

Marone! I was going to need a fresh hankie. I was going to need a bed sheet. "Don't you mean to say that Kyle took out the gun?"

"No."

"Maybe you argued, the two of you struggled for the gun and it went off accidentally?"

"Oh no. I shot him on purpose."

"How many? How many times did you shoot him?"

"I don't remember."

Geez girlie! This wasn't brain surgery! If it was I would have signed you up for a transplant.

"The police report says you emptied the gun, did you?"

"No... maybe... if they say so."

"What do *you* say?"

"It was all so crazy! I'd never shot a gun before. It was loud and scary, it jumped in my hand and hurt my shoulder. I closed my eyes and just kept pulling the trigger!"

"And when it was over, you dropped the gun and ran out?"

"Yessssss."

"But first you wiped your prints off the gun?"

Sissy looked at me as if this was new information. She stared at me a beat before finally saying "Yes."

"And nobody saw this? This whole time it was just you and Kyle in the room, no room service waiter, no cleaning lady no Marshall, nobody?"

"Yessssss! Oh God, what did I do? What did I do?"

And with that she broke down in tears, beating me to it by seconds. I scratched my chin and watched her sob, her top-heavy body weaving back and forth like an upside down pendulum. I began to fear for the glass coffee table.

But the tears seemed genuine, and it was the first time that night the girl had showed any emotion at all. Maybe I was being too rough on her. Maybe the poor kid was still in shock. Sure, that was it, she wasn't as brainless as sea brine, she was simply dazed and in shock. I should have cut her some slack and I felt lousy.

"Zolly," she said, drawing her hands from her reddened eyes. "I know I did a terrible terrible thing. But do you think, do you think it will, will..?" She was choking on tears. "Do you think it will hurt my career?"

Wha?! Her career?! Bells were ringing again as my head clapped back and forth. What career was she talking about? The one as a "D" list celebrity bouncing around a jungle in a wet bikini on some third rate TV reality show? The career highlighted by eating bugs and running a three legged race through pond scum tied to a former child star with a coke addiction?! Not to digress, but this is the difference between Americans and the English. In England if someone wants to become an actor, they join a repertory company and practice their art for years and years in the many excellent regional theaters. They hone their craft playing everything from Shakespeare to Ibsen to Neil Simon. In America if you want to become an actor you get a boob job and eat a bug. But don't get me started.

I turned to the pathetic creature before me and spoke with the utmost sincerity. "Sweetie, I don't think there's anything that could hurt your career."

CHAPTER FIVE

I left Sissy's room feeling like I had just stepped off a merry-go-round spinning out of control. The girl was hopeless. I'd given her every opportunity to latch onto a defense, but she wouldn't bite. It also bothered me that she seemed more concerned about her career than the guy she was going to marry lying dead in the morgue. I didn't see one tear shed for the poor schlub. No wonder he was breaking it off. But was it because he realized his future wife was as cold and dim as the bottom of a well during an eclipse? It shouldn't have taken him as long as it did to figure that out.

Nah, maybe there was some other reason. A reason Sissy didn't want me to know. Maybe it was the usual thing; he got tired of Tits on a Stick and went after the fast food special of the month. Maybe Sissy got wise to this and that's why she killed him. Bingo! I just provided her motive. Good work Zolly.

On the other hand it was probably giving Sissy too much credit to believe she could pre-meditate anything. Maybe the guy wasn't cheating on her, maybe he simply figured out that marrying Sissy wasn't going to be the ride on Ariélle's gravy train he thought it would. Ariélle was way too smart to hand over her fortune to another trainer/entrepreneur. She'd been there, done that.

And what about this J-Up character? Was he as harmless as Sissy believed? He had warned that if he couldn't have her no one could. Maybe in his delusional mind he actually became the gangster he imagined himself and killed Kyle out of a mad passion to keep Sissy for himself. Or maybe it was for revenge, or to maintain his image. Who knows what goes on in the minds of these people? They probably don't know themselves. And if you want to know who's to blame I'll tell you. TV soap operas. Yeah, soap operas. Watch six hours a day of people on their twelfth marriage lying, cheating and backstabbing to satisfy their lust for sex and money – and sooner or later you begin to accept what you see as civilized behavior. Add to the soaps all those sleazy talk shows where fist fights break out over which of three guys is the real father of some poor unwed mother's fifth kid, and well, you've pretty much glorified what used to be called "immorality." But don't get me started.

My regret of the day was not talking to J-Up in the hotel corridor when I had the chance. Of course then I didn't know he'd become one of my prime suspects. He certainly had motive. The only thing that didn't make sense was why if J-Up killed her fiancée Sissy would confess to the murder? Was she still in love with the guy and trying to protect him? And if not J-Up, who *was* Sissy protecting? Maybe the simplest answer was the truest – Sissy killed Kyle as she claimed.

By the time I realized I needed to question Mr. J-Up he had disappeared from the hotel. Sissy didn't have a current address for him, guessing he usually spent the night with whatever die hard groupie brought him to her bed after his last show. Not that there were a lot of shows anymore.

She gave me his cell phone number and remarkably he was still paying the bill and it was in service. The problem was he wasn't answering it. After half a dozen unreturned calls I finally left a message: "Hey, yeah, J-Up, it's good to talk to you man. My name is Blaine Collins of Collins Entertainment. I manage a bunch of clubs in the Midwest and I'd like to discuss hiring you for some gigs. I'm a big fan." I left my phone number in the mouse trap but didn't get any immediate bites.

While I was on the phone I took the opportunity to check out the witnesses from the sixth floor of the Babylon who claimed to have heard the gun shots. I started with the guy from Indiana. I was surprised to find him real choked up about the murder. "Death is a horrible thing. You never know when it's coming," he said in a voice full of doom and gloom. "Are you prepared Mr. Michelangelo?" He then proceeded to try and sell me a life insurance policy. Geez!

In-between his descriptions of the multitude of ways I might be snatched from this earth at any moment, I was finally able to confirm pretty much what the police had already gotten from the guy. He'd heard gun shots sometime before Eleven A.M.

Next I called the honeymoon couple back home in Philadelphia. The phone was answered by the groom and as soon as he heard what my business was he got very nervous and started acting suspiciously. When pressed he admitted the story he'd given the police wasn't exactly the truth. He confessed that he wasn't exactly on his honeymoon and that the woman he was with wasn't exactly his wife. If his real wife should find out he'd be exactly in deep shit.

I told the guy I had no desire to get him in trouble and promised not to call him at home again if he cooperated fully. This calmed him down and he went on to recall what happened the day of the murder. After being awakened by gunshots he jumped up in bed, glanced at the alarm clock and noticed it was eight minutes before Eleven. I asked why he didn't report the gunshots immediately and he said he didn't want to stick his nose in something that might expose the fact he was sticking another body part in somebody not his wife.

I believed the guy even though he was a proven liar, maybe because he had no reason to lie about the time of the shots. And maybe because with all the lusting I was doing over Ariélle I could imagine myself in a similar situation with Tina. I'd like to believe I wasn't that kind of guy. But I'd also like to believe you can lose weight on an "All Chocolate" diet.

My next move was to check out the scene of the crime. After literally greasing the wheels of justice with a couple more meatball subs to Slowicki he took me to Sissy's old room in the Babylon where the killing took place. I was surprised but not too surprised that there was no yellow police tape across the door, and Slowicki explained the management of the Babylon thought that might spook the other guests. So with a phone call to a well-placed friend in the mayor's office the tape was dispensed with. Isn't it grand how our legal system works? "Justice for All," if by that you mean "all the rich guys."

While Slowicki went off to get some exercise tapping the button on a slot machine I gave the place a look over. This wasn't a grand suite like Ariélle's, just your standard hotel room. Sissy probably could have done better in one of the more deluxe rooms of Mommy's penthouse, but who wants Mommy on the other side of the door when you're shacking up with your boyfriend?

I entered the door into a little hall with a clothes closet on the left and the bathroom on the right. Moving past these I peered into the main living area. Sissy was right. The room was messy. Murder messy. My nostrils flared.

On the wall to the right a queen bed was flanked by a couple of oval shaped nightstands. The bed was unmade, its blanket and sheets twisted to the floor as if someone had slept in it. Or done something fun in it. The drawer on the nightstand to the right of the bed, closest to me, was half open. Opposite the bed on the left wall was a dresser with a lamp and a TV. The screen of the TV was shattered in a pattern resembling a spider web, but considering the crap on TV nowadays that was probably a blessing. Beyond this, in front of the windows, was a sitting area. A round cherry table with a couple of straight back chairs was tucked in a corner to the left. On the table top was a plastic container holding tourist brochures, a beige telephone, and several shards of white glass. I looked up and saw the remaining half of what was once a globe light suspended over the table from a chain. To the right of this an armchair and love seat were arranged in an L shaped pattern.

"Huh," I said to myself, clucking my tongue. Tits on a Stick was right about shooting blindly. She managed to take out the TV on the left and the globe light close to the ceiling a good six feet away. In fact, the room was sprayed with bullets. Little yellow forensic flags marking where slugs had been removed were widely scattered across the walls and ceiling.

I stepped into the living area and the hairs inside my nostrils began to do the rumba. Blood. On the carpet near the round table was a large stain the color of dark rubies. Someone had bled a lot.

Lifting my glance, I turned slowly in a circle, taking it all in. My eyes stopped on the open drawer of the nightstand on the far side of the bed. Circling the bed I walked to the nightstand and looked back. It had to be at least fifteen feet.

If Sissy had taken the gun from this drawer and shot from this spot she would have had to be very lucky to send a round through her fiancée's heart. Or should I say, very *unlucky.* Huh.

Something was off. I looked around the room again and noticed some fancy perfume bottles scattered across the dresser. Beside them were combs and a couple hairbrushes. I picked one up and found strands of what looked like Sissy's naturally Blonde hair - complete with black roots. But who am I to be catty? Me with the lifts in my shoes. Jesus, did I just admit that? Keep it quiet, will ya?

I set the hairbrush down on the dresser beside a platinum framed photo of Ariélle with her arm wrapped around a young Sissy. It was one of the few existing photographs in which I'd ever seen Ariélle smiling.

You gotta be a real snoop in my business and I make no apologies. I spent the next few minutes poking through the dresser drawers and found the usual women's clothing: panties, bras, shorts, tees. Sliding open a bottom drawer I heard something roll back and forth and my snoop-ometer went off. Under a couple unopened packages of pantyhose I found - a dildo. A big dildo. Coiled beside it was a black plastic belt with a hole in it. I think when you attached the dildo through the hole you got what they call a "strap-on." I must of picked the term up in some medical journal or something in my doctor's waiting room. I delicately slid the drawer shut without further investigation. Who was I to judge what kind of kinky, sick, disgusting stuff Sissy and her fiancée were into?

As I searched the room further a definite pattern began to develop. I checked out the closets and discovered them stuffed with women's clothing. On the bathroom counter I found an assortment of lip sticks, cosmetics, wrinkle creams and cellulite fighters - the best snake oil some over-the-hill ex-TV star could pedal for a thousand per cent mark up. Rich women bought them in crystal decanters on Rodeo Drive at five hundred bucks a pop, and poor women got theirs off the Home Shopping Network for nineteen ninety-five, proving human nature is human nature, and that Barnum was wrong. There are a *million* suckers born every minute.

Yeah there was a definite pattern here. Not of things I found in the room, but of what I didn't find. No men's things. No clothes. No razor, shaving cream, after shave... zilch.

It was odd. Sure Kyle the trainer lived here in Atlantic City and had his own place. But you'd think there would be some evidence he was spending at least some nights in Sissy's room. Maybe Sissy was saving herself for marriage. It was possible. Yeah, right. It was also possible I could put on a bikini and be crowned Miss America.

I closed the door behind me and walked down the corridor of the hotel pondering these questions. I was also pondering whether to have a couple slices of pepperoni on the boardwalk or drive back home and grab dinner with Tina. As fate would have it the matter was settled when my cell phone rang and it was Tina.

"Zolly, are you alright? Why didn't you call me?"

"I'm fine baby; I just got caught up with some things and haven't had the time to check in."

"Did you meet Ariélle? Is she still as sexy as ever?"

"Sexy? To tell the truth I didn't notice. I'm trying to keep it professional, you know?" Okay, it was a little white lie. Like Moby Dick was a little white whale. But I was only lying to protect Tina. What was I going to tell her, that Ariélle remained the sexiest woman on the planet and I still had the hots for her? Now don't get me wrong, it's not like Tina's the jealous type. If she ever caught me with another woman she wouldn't say anything - except maybe "oops" after she dropped a grand piano on my head.

"So, Zol, when are you coming home? I've got something special in the oven for you."

"Really, babe, what did you make?"

"I got this recipe from the American Heart Association for a real low-fat broccoli and tuna casserole." Broccoli and tuna versus pizza? The pondering was over.

"I'm sorry, Hon, but I'm gonna be at this awhile. You should eat without me." I felt like a rat. Here I was lusting after another woman and betraying the American Heart Association.

"Okay Zol. But you take care of yourself. I've still got a bad feeling about this case."

I was beginning to wonder if Tina was really psychic. Was the "bad feeling" she was getting more about my lusting after Ariélle than about my personal safety? After hanging up I made a pledge to myself to be a better person and to make it up to Tina for lying. Besides, it was all a fantasy. There was no way in Hell anything could happen between a woman like Ariélle and a schlub like me. And even on the remote chance in a million it did, I was sure I couldn't cheat on Tina. Well, almost sure.

I set back down the corridor to drown my guilt in mozzarella. Almost at the elevators I passed an open door to a guest room and heard the groan of a vacuum cleaner. Being a snoop I looked in and saw a Hispanic housekeeper punishing the floor with a Hoover. I recalled Slowicki saying the cops had questioned a maid who was working on the floor the day of the murder. She said she hadn't seen anything, but as long as I had the opportunity I thought I'd talk to her myself. Sometimes cops can miss little things – like the eruption of Kilimanjaro.

"Excuse me, Ma'am," I said, entering the room and getting a better look at the housekeeper. She was a squat Hispanic woman whose body type could best be described as "fire plug." Her coarse gray hair was pulled back and tied with some kind of black velvet twist; and her face was layered with wrinkles like a wall of the Grand Canyon.

"Perdonome," the woman said, a little startled. She must have thought this was my room. "Lo siento mucho. Vuelvo," she said starting for the door.

"No, no, it's bueno. Do you speak English?" She shook her head "no" and I knew I was in trouble. I'd made an effort to learn Spanish, but I just don't have a facility for foreign languages. I have enough trouble understanding Arnold Schwarzenegger. "Espera…espere.. uno menudo," I said, asking her to "wait one soup."

I took out my cell phone and called one of my life-lines.

"Victor's Tacos," a voice answered.

"Victor?"

"Oh, Senor Zolly, do you know you left your sunglasses here?"

"Thanks, I'll come by for 'em. Listen, Victor, I was wondering if you could help me out." For the next ten minutes Mirabelle and I passed the phone back and forth like two giggling girls at a sleep-over making prank calls. I'd ask a question, Victor would translate it to her, then translate her answer back to me. It boggles my mind that a satellite in outer space was necessary for two people standing next to each other to have a conversation.

I asked Mirabelle if she normally worked this floor and if the police had questioned her about the murder. She said "yes" and that she had already told the police she didn't see anything. Now she may have been talking in Spanish, but the human face speaks a universal language. I could see she was troubled and not telling the truth. When persuaded she told me about her "stick up the ass" boss and the fear that she'd be fired. I promised her that the conversation was strictly between the two – or well, three of us -and promised that I wouldn't let anyone fire her for telling the truth.

I guess there's something about me that people trust, because Mirabelle confessed that while she normally worked this, the sixth floor, the day of the murder a friend filled in for her so she could take her granddaughter to the dentist. She didn't think it would be a problem since her friend was also a housekeeper here at the Babylon and her boss was always bragging how he could never tell any of them apart.

After pledging again that no one was going to lose their job, Mirabelle agreed that she wanted to do the right thing, and gave me her friend Guadalupe's phone number. On my way out, when she wasn't looking I slipped a twenty onto the dresser. A little gift from the Tooth Fairy.

CHAPTER SIX

On the drive home I tried calling the number Mirabelle gave me a bunch of times but got no answer. Now I had two people not returning my calls. I was beginning to feel as unpopular as a telemarketer selling root canals. Of course there was no reason to take it personally. J-Up might have been busy signing autographs, or too high to trace the ringing sound to the small device in his pocket. Guadalupe might have at least had a good excuse. Maybe she, like most of the immigrants coming here, was busy working two jobs. Or maybe her friend had warned her off me. Sure I had promised to protect them, but would you jeopardize the food in your kid's mouth to help a stranger?

When I got back to Seaside I thought for a minute about grabbing a cone on the boardwalk for dessert, but I was actually too tired to eat. That in itself was an exceptional event worthy of being marked on the calendar. But it had been a long and frustrating day. I decided instead to retreat to the cozy cocoon of my apartment.

I live in a great two-story building a couple of blocks off the boardwalk. Painted Miami pink it's got broad covered porches lined with white balustrades. The grand old place was built during the heyday of the Jersey Shore resorts before jet travel made it easier to get to places like Miami or the Caribbean. From my second story porch I can lie on my aluminum chaise and feel the soothing ocean breeze sweep over my body. During the day I'm hypnotized by the rhythmic breaking of waves on the beach. At night I can watch the colored lights of the honky-tonk boardwalk glitter before me. It's also a great place for people watching. And I'm not just talking about people in bikinis, because trust me, there are a hell of a lot of people wearing bikinis who shouldn't be.

Grabbing a Diet Coke from the fridge I headed out to my heavenly observation deck. I left the porch light off to keep things mellow and plopped on the chaise.

"Ahh! Ahh!!!! Help!!!" came a shriek out of the darkness. I felt arms and legs writhing and flailing under me and jumped to my feet to slap on the porch light. On the chaise a frightened creature stared up at me - eyes wide, chest heaving. Then as a look of recognition crossed its face the heaving subsided.

"Zolly?" Tina gasped.

"It's okay, it's okay, it's me babe," I said, rushing over and wrapping my arms around her. "Are you okay, sweetie?"

"Yeah, I'm fine Zol."

"Baby, what the hell are you doing sitting here in the dark?"

"I must have fell asleep. I thought you might be hungry so I've been keeping the casserole warm in the oven for you."

"Ah, you're the best." I rewarded her with a kiss on the cheek. She *was* the best. Always thinking of me. And here I was all day thinking of nothing but Ariélle. I was back in Ratsville where I belonged. But it spurred me to think. It was time to do the right thing. "Listen, Tina, sit down, I've got something to say." Tina sat in a webbed lawn chair, looking concerned.

"I know, you hate broccoli, but Zol you've gotta..."

"Ssh," I whispered, taking her hand softly in mine and getting down on one knee.

"Oh God Zolly! Are you having a heart attack?! Oh God I dreaded this day!!"

"No, no, no babe. I'm down here on purpose. I'm feeling fine. In fact, I've never felt better in my life. And you know why?"

"Why, Zol?"

"Because I'm tired of all this temporary stuff. Of you living in your place and me in mine. Of us being together and not together."

"Oh Zolly!" The concern deepened on her face.

"Babe, I want..." Shit. I was doing this all wrong. I didn't even have a ring or anything to give her. I searched my pants pocket hoping to find who knows what and found my car keys. Eureka! That little metal hoop from the valet ticket was still on them. I quickly pried it off and slipped it onto Tina's finger.

Damn I'm cool under pressure. "Baby, I want you to be my wife."

Tina stared down at the improvised engagement ring on her finger like Superman looking at Kryptonite. "Dammit Zolly!" she swore, and Tina rarely swears. "Why are you doing this to me?!"

I have to admit, her acting as if I were persecuting her got me a little miffed. And when I'm miffed I get sarcastic. "Gee, I don't know babe, I thought I could promise you a lifetime of pain and misery."

"That's just what I'd get!" she moaned, jumping out of the chair and gripping the railing with her back to me.

"C'mon, Baby." I moved to her and tenderly began rubbing her back.

"No, you c'mon, Zolly. How many times have do we have to go through this?"

Did I mention that I had already proposed to Tina six times? But I wasn't giving up. I leaned in close to her ear and spoke softly. "You know how much I love you."

"And you know how much I love you, you shit! How *could* you ask me to marry you?!"

Okay, maybe an explanation is in order. You see, Tina's a great girl. She's warm and caring, fun and unselfish - not to mention sexy as hell. The problem is she's just a little gun-shy after a bad divorce. Well, three bad divorces actually. Now I wasn't there and didn't know the guys, but I can't imagine that whatever went wrong was Tina's fault. Unfortunately that's all

Tina could imagine. And although she really loved me, she was afraid that the surest way to kill that love would be to marry me.

"Okay, okay. I apologize for trying to make you happy," I said sincerely, turning her around so we were face to face. "And I promise never to do it again."

"Really?" Tina wiped the tears from her eyes.

"Trust me, from now on I'm 'Mr. Non-Commitment.' There ain't no way I'm gonna do the right thing."

"Oh, Zolly! You're the best!" Tina gushed, throwing her arms around me. Once again all was right with the universe.

CHAPTER SEVEN

I woke up the next morning with a look of un-wedded bliss smeared across my face. Who ever thought promising not to marry somebody would turn them into an animal in bed. I swaggered into the kitchen, the proud stallion relishing his conquest. Tina was already off to one of her multiple jobs, but left a post-it note with smiley faces and hearts on the fridge door. Do I know how to please a woman or not?

I called Guadalupe's number again before and after my shower, but still got no answer. So I headed over to the personnel office at the Babylon. Excuse me, I headed over to the Human Resources Office at the Babylon. That's what they call it nowadays. "Personnel Office" was too clear and to the point. "Human Resources" sounded more important, but I never liked the term. "Resources." It made it sound like people were some kind of ore to be mined. It also reminded me of that old sci-fi flick *Soylent Green*. At the end the police detective discovers the mystery food the government is feeding people is actually made out of dead humans. "Soylent Green is people!" Charlton Heston screams in shock. Now there was

an actor. And to my knowledge he never once donned a wet
bikini or ate a bug.

At the Babylon I avoided the valet attendant and headed
straight to "self-parking." The extra walking more than made
up for the insults, and the tip I saved helped defer the cost of
the box of pastries under my arm. Torture? Truth serum? I've
found nothing works better in an interrogation than good old
Dunkin' Donuts.

I made my way into the bowels of the hotel to a no
man's land guests aren't meant to see. Here a maze of tunnels
connected all the hidden essentials of a small city – the kitchens,
laundries, garbage storage, security offices and power plant. Lit
by fluorescent lights that gave off an eerie glow and high pitched
buzz, the tunnels were lined with pipes and exposed electrical
wiring and always smelled like sour milk. Uniformed security
and maintenance men whizzed back and forth on golf carts like
in some futuristic megalopolis. A perfect setting for Human
Resources.

As is my practice I arrived at the office fifteen minutes
before it was scheduled to open. A small window of time
usually exists between the time some janitor schlub unlocks
the door and the person occupying the office drags themselves
in for another day at the salt mines.

As I sat in a colorful plastic shell chair waiting for
somebody to arrive, I noticed a secretary had left her
computer on overnight. I considered that an invitation to sit

in her more comfortable desk chair and casually browse the employee database for one Guadalupe Zelaya.

"Can I help you?" The stern and annoyed voice startled me and I looked up over the computer monitor like a dog caught chewing its master's slipper. Before me stood a woman I would best describe as "substantial." I'm not saying she was fat or even very tall, just solid. Closing in on sixty, she had the look of experience and authority of one who has risen through the ranks of their profession. She wore sensible black pumps, an officious gray tweed pantsuit, and her hair in a bun. This bureaucratic image was softened somewhat by a kind face lightly made up with powder and blush. In deference to her substantial appearance I will from this point on refer to her as "Helen From Human Resources, or H.F.H.R."

"Excuse me?" H.F.H.R. said, attempting to capture my attention again. It was time for "Mr. Charm." I don't know what it is, my smile, my non-threatening regular-guy looks, or maybe my stylish fedora; but I can be pretty damn charming when I want to. Women find me irresistible and it's sad to say but I sometimes take advantage of it. It didn't hurt that Helen was a single woman on the cusp of becoming an old lady and that she liked donuts.

"Oh I'm so sorry," I said, quickly rising from the chair. "This is truly embarrassing, but my cell phone isn't working and I was just using your computer to check my email. It's totally inexcusable, but you see in my business there's always something urgent popping up."

"Who are you?" H.F.H.R. asked, still a little wary.

"Oh, god, excuse my manners." I'm Agent Michelangelo from the state lottery commission." I handed her a business card.

"How can I help you Mr. Michelangelo?" she asked coolly.

"Well, for starters you can call me Zolly. And then if I'm not being too presumptuous you can have a donut with me. I apologize again, but I didn't have a chance to grab breakfast. I got a tip and came right over." I held the box of donuts up and opened the lid with a flourish like a model on a TV game show displaying a chest full of golden treasure.

"Well, I was planning on being good and just having my coffee," H.F.H.R. said, glancing down guiltily at the Styrofoam cup of coffee in her hand. "But I don't suppose one would hurt" she said with a small laugh.

"Good, good." I ushered her into a chair opposite me at the desk. I flourished the box lid once again and she made a selection. "Ah, a glazed maple bar, you're a woman after my own heart."

A couple of donuts a piece later Helen and I were getting pretty chummy. Donuts have the power to do that. I always say if the world had more donuts and less whole wheat bread we'd all get along a lot better. In short time I learned that Helen's favorite dessert was custard, she loved Cocker Spaniels, and gardening. She'd been very successful raising violets, though she sometimes felt guilty for devoting so much time to them. When I asked if there was a man in her life she blushed and confessed she'd had a couple close calls but remained a single woman. "That's hard to believe," I said, "how could a woman as charming and attractive as you have escaped us men for so long?"

Okay, okay, I'm a rat, I've already admitted that. You can question my methods but just remember the time may come when you need my help to find a lost loved one or defend yourself from false charges. Let's see how judgmental you are then.

Eventually H.F.H.R. and I got around to discussing the reason I had come to see her. Blushing a little myself I told her I would have come a lot sooner had I known what a charming young lady I would be dealing with. After choking on a chocolate cream-filled, or my own guile, I told Helen I was from the State Lottery Commission's investigative unit. We were having trouble locating one of her employees, a Miss or Mrs. Guadalupe Zelaya. The lucky woman had hit a twenty-five hundred dollar jackpot but somehow her claim form got chewed up by our equipment and Guadalupe's address and phone number were lost.

H.F.H.R. was sympathetic but reluctantly informed me it was against company policy to release employee information without a court order. I praised the policy but shook my head, despairing that by the time we worked our way through the courts the deadline for Guadalupe claiming her prize would have passed. It was such a shame, I was sure Guadalupe was hard working and the twenty-five hundred dollars could be a real help to her. Perhaps she'd be able to bring an aging mother up from El Salvador, or send money home for food and much needed medical care. "I can see you're a compassionate and caring human being, Helen. The kind of person I wished I could meet more often," I said, giving her my sad dog eyes. "It's not your fault that bureaucratic rules are going to cause a real human tragedy."

Guadalupe's apartment building was built in 1937 and meticulously maintained until 1938. It was in the slum section of Atlantic City – a section that included the ninety-eight per cent of the city behind the boardwalk. One of the arguments for legalizing gambling was how it would renew the city and help the poor. Well someone was pocketing billions of dollars, but it sure never found its way here. Funny how no one ever questions it. But don't get me started.

There was a parking space right in front of the building, but I didn't like the looks of the old Ford LTD to the rear. You could bet this boat was driven by a little old lady who could barely see over the dash board, the kind who would plow into the bumper of my beautiful Mini Cooper and not even realize it. So I parked two blocks out of my way just to be safe. I got out of ruby red beauty, closed the door and had a heart attack. Falling to my knees I clutched the door handle.

Was that a scratch? Squatting and eyeballing it in horror, I grasped my chest then sighed in relief. It was a hair. A dog hair. Probably from my neighbor Mrs. Goodman's Chow. She was going to have to be more fastidious about grooming or I was going to have to find a new place to park.

Recovering from the myocardial infarction, I dragged my ass up three flights of stairs thinking I was going to have a real heart attack and vowing on my mother's grave I was gonna let Tina put me on that low-fat diet. At the top I found myself in a cave-like hallway lined with heavy mahogany doors and dark paneling. To accent all the dark wood the walls and carpeting were a cheerful dark chocolate color. Overall you got the impression you were in a mole hole. To add to the ambience the whole place smelled of aging shellac. Between wheezes I knocked on Guadalupe's apartment door. No one answered. I listened and thought I heard someone moving inside, so I knocked again.

A door to the next apartment creaked opened a crack and what I think was a female face asked me what I wanted. As soon as I mentioned the name "Guadalupe" the face told me "She went back to El Salvador" and the door closed in my face. Now it may have been true Guadalupe had moved, or it may have been that this was the standard thing said to a white man in a sport coat who looked like he might be an immigration officer or bill collector. I was pretty sure I had heard something inside Guadalupe's apartment, so I called on one of my old tricks for checking whether somebody is coming or going from a place. I pulled a flyer out of my jacket that had a photo of an adorable calico cat and the words "Fluffy needs a home!"

The trick was to place the flyer outside a door and check back later to see if it was still there. If it wasn't, it was a good bet somebody had come out of the apartment and picked it up. And if I got real lucky they might even call the phone number on the flyer and I'd be talking to who I was after. I always carried a few flyers with me. It was a beautiful plan. And it finally provided a reason for cats to exist on this planet. Whoa. Okay, I'm not gonna say anything bad about cats because I know what shit that will get me into. Let me just say I never understood why people love these cuddly, adorable kitties who have fangs only a few evolutionary steps away from those of the Saber Tooth Tiger.

I bent down to place the bait, and while at it tried to peek through the crack under the door. It was at that point I heard what Moses must have heard when God spoke to him on Mt. Sinai. A deep, awe inspiring voice that echoed like rolling thunder: "Can I help you?" Still bent over, with the cat flyer in hand, I pivoted and found myself staring at the biggest pair of shoes I'd ever seen. Paul Bunyan's feet could swim inside these babies.

My eyes drifted up two tree trunks clad in gray khaki to a torso as thick as a redwood. Sticking out like branches were arms with biceps that looked like steel drums bulging with pressure and about to burst. "Looking for something?" the voice boomed sternly. I stood up and found myself eye level with the belt buckle of a very large man of African-American persuasion. Faced with a situation like this possums play dead. My usual M.O. was to cover my mug with the huge dopey grin of an idiot. No one's threatened by an idiot. More important, no one wants to hurt them.

"Can I have some candy, Daddy?" I heard a small sugary voice behind Paul Bunyon. The cutest little girl in pink bunny pajamas had slipped out the open door to their apartment.

"You already had enough," the giant called firmly down to her without taking his eyes off me.

"But Dad-eeeeeeeee," she whined, wrapping her arms around one of his tree trunks.

"Okay, Baby, anything you want." His voice suddenly turned as gentle as a kindergarten teacher's. It was obvious she was wrapped around his leg and he was wrapped around her little finger.

"What's that Daddy?" the adorable little voice asked, her tiny finger pointing to the flyer in my hand.

"Yeah, what is it?" the voice demanded.

"Uh, well, it's a cat. You see I found this stray and I'm trying to find it a good home."

"Can I have the kitty, Daddy, please... pleaseeeeeee," the sugar plumb cajoled, ripping the flyer from my hand.

"Sure, Baby," her father answered. "Give her the cat."

"Uh, well, you see, that could be a problem."

"My Baby wants the cat. Can you think of one good reason why my Baby isn't going to get the cat?"

I stared at the veins rippling on his eyeballs. They were almost as big as the ones rippling on his biceps, and said "No reason at all."

Here's a tip for you. If you've ever thought about putting a cat on a leash, don't. I can't stress this enough, don't. Twenty minutes later I was walking out of the local S.P.C.A. with Mr. Fangs, a creature part cat, part kangaroo, part super ball, part Satan. What do I know about cats? I'm a dog person, so I put him on a leash. It was like tying a rope to a lightning bolt. Up! Down! Sideways! Horizontal! Vertical! My arm extended out from my body like the hour hand on an insane clock. All the time the rope was digging into my hand, cutting off the flow of blood. Bim! Bam! Three o'clock! Six o'clock! Two o'clock! Nine o'clock! Twelve-thirty! Bing! Boom! Zip! I had never seen a living thing bounce like that. My eyeballs ached just trying to keep up with it. My fingers were going numb but not numb enough to miss the sting of the rope burns.

Twenty minutes and a dozen attempts later I had exhausted Mr. Fangs and somehow managed to stuff the Hell cat into my precious Mini-Cooper. Then like a Special Forces soldier parachuting into enemy territory I jumped in behind the wheel and slammed the door shut before the Devil's spawn could escape. I managed all this with only six additional fang punctures to my hand, ankles, and neck.

But that didn't end it. Devil Cat's wild ride continued
inside the car as he bounced around like a ping pong ball
in a bingo machine. Front seat! Back seat! Door! Headrest!
Ceiling! Dashboard! Finally - floor well. There he froze.
Was he exhausted or merely planning a new attack? I stared
at him. He stared at me. And that's when it happened.
Armageddon.

Apparently Mr. Fangs had never read the Geneva Accords
because he suddenly screeched like a banshee and let loose a
chemical attack. Right there! On the beautifully shampooed
and meticulously groomed carpet of my shiny spotless Mini
Cooper. The pride of my life! Sprayed with cat piss!!! Is there
anything worse?! I have never in my entire life have felt so
violated.

At that moment my cell phone rang, and after regaining
the will to live I answered it. "Hel-lo," I stammered as the
veins on my forehead began to do the Tango. It was Helen,
the matronly lady from Human Resources at the Babylon.
As part of the con to get Guadalupe's address I'd given her a
business card with my phone number, not thinking she'd ever
use it. "Oh, hi Helen... yeah, it's nice to hear from you too
dear, but to tell you the truth this isn't a good time... No, no,
I wasn't being insincere when I said you had nice teeth, it's
just that at this moment I.... what? This Saturday night? Uh,
I'll have to check my calendar... but no, I swear I wasn't using
you Darling, I'd never do that.... good, good, I feel the same

way, it was fate... Okay, I promise, I'll check and I'll get back to you real soon."

Like many victims of hellish traumas, I blocked out much of what happened next. I retain hazy images of dragging the cat up three flights of stairs and delivering it to Paul Bunyan. Fangs continued his Cirque du Soleil acrobatics the entire time and to this day I still shudder and begin to perspire when I recall the voice of the giant telling me I'd have to take the cat back because it was too wild. I remember debating what would be easier: throwing the cat out the window or simply jumping out myself. Luckily I was saved when the sweet little girl picked up the devil-cat, it licked her face sweetly, and the Sequoia Tree said "Okay. We'll keep him."

The next thing I remember clearly was glancing at the door to Guadalupe's alleged apartment. The cat flyer I'd had the presence of mind to place there during my earlier departure was gone. Maybe the sugar plumb fairy took it. Or maybe the janitor. Or maybe Guadalupe was still living there.

After several trips through the car wash I found myself outside her door again, this time holding a large pizza. I knocked on the door and in an anonymous voice barked "Pizza." Nothing. I knocked again, nothing. Finally I shouted "Oh my God! Is it? I think it is! I see the face of Our Lady in the pizza cheese! Santa Maria! It's a miracle!"

The door swung open and I was eyeball to eyeball with a force of nature named Guadalupe Zelaya. Guadalupe was a pretty petite Latina in her twenties. She had a pony tail and bangs that drew your attention to a pair of eyes blazing with intensity. She could best be described as lightning in a bottle. Her diminutive body contained a wellspring of boundless energy. The woman didn't walk, she bounced; her feet attacking the earth and defying gravity. "Are jou Mr. Zolly?" she asked in a friendly voice that had an endearing squeakiness and thick Latin accent.

"Yeah, look, I'm sorry for having to trick you with the pizza thing, but I really need to talk to you."

"Jou don't trick me. Mirabelle called and told me jou were a good guy and it was okay to talk to jou. If jou had just said jou were Mr. Zolly I would have answered the door right away."

Saint Guadalupe invited me in and tended to my cat wounds with antiseptic and band-aids. Her small apartment didn't have much furniture but we sat cozily on some pillows on the floor with the pizza between us and ate. The woman had the body of a bird but the appetite of a wolverine. I could have fallen in love with her right then and there had I not already had Tina and Ariélle in my romance queue.

I chomped down on a slice knowing I was in serious competition here and would have to keep up the pace if I was going to claim my half of the pizza. With a string of cheese stretching from my lips to the slice I asked Guadalupe about the day Kyle Broder was killed. "So you were working Mirabelle's shift on the floor where the murder took place?"

"Jes, I was." She sprinkled some salt on her pizza.

"Did you notice anything strange going on that afternoon?"

"Strange? Jou won't believe what kinda strange things jou see working in a hotel like that." Guadalupe talked about a hundred miles an hour but was able to chew at the same time. Her eyes rolled as she looked back on something from her past. "There was this one time I walk into a room and this man who had to be three hundred pounds, and so hairy, yuck; he's lying on the bed naked except for a baby... a baby... oh damn, what do you call a hat the niño wears?" She was frustrated that her mastery of English had not yet caught up with the speed of her mind.

"Bonnet. I think you're talking about a baby bonnet."

"Jes, a bonnet, he is wearing nothing but this bonnet and a big diaper. Then he has the cojones to offers me fifty dollars to spank him. Santa Catarina! Can you believe that?"

"Brother, it's a mixed up world." My eyes scrunched as I tried to exorcize the image of the three hundred pound infant from my mind.

"Jour telling me. Another time I'm cleaning a room and I hear this squealing coming from the bathroom. I open the door and there in the bathtub is a cerdito!" She burst into laughter and I felt jealous that I couldn't understand what she'd said.

"A what?"

"Un cerdito!" she answered. Then, seeing that I didn't understand she searched for the English translation. "Uh, un jamon... un porky!" She put her finger on her ass, curled it up, and oinked like a pig.

"A pig!" I shouted as if I'd just won a game of charades.

"Si, a pig. But not just a pig, he was wearing a sweater, I swear to jou, a red sweater with the name of a school on it. I think, jes, it said 'Harvard.' And he was so angry and making so much noise!"

"Maybe he was angry because he was a Yale man."

"Oh, so you've seen this before? Pigs in sweaters? Is that like a piñata for a holiday or something? I swear I am never going to learn everything I need to know about this country."

"No, no, I was just making a joke."

"Oh, jou are laughing at me?"

"No, no, not at 'jou' – I mean 'you'."

"Because if jou are laughing at me I think jou owe me that last slice of pepperoni. Why would jou order a pizza with pepperoni on only half?"

"Uh, I wasn't sure if you'd like pepperoni. But if you want the last piece it's yours." Remember this day well; you won't hear me say something like that again for the remainder of your life.

Guadalupe took me up on my offer and separated the remaining piece of pepperoni from the rest of the pizza in the box. "Next time get extra cheese," she said, taking a voracious bite. She wasn't joking. I could have sat with her all afternoon listening to stories about the strange goings on in hotels, but I felt obligated to get back to the little business of a dead guy.

"So Guadalupe, what I need to know is, the day we were talking about - were you working anywhere near room 652?"

"I was all around the 600's, jes, plus downstairs in the 5's. I was going back and forth," she answered, wiping some pizza oil from her chin.

"Did you notice anything out of the ordinary happening around room 652? And I'm not talking Ivy League pigs."

"I don't know what this 'ivory league' thing is, but I didn't see nothing unusual."

"Well okay, did you hear anything?"

"I try not to listen. Jou wouldn't sleep at night if you hear the things I hear in the hotel. Jou won't believe the noises I hear coming out of human peoples."

I paused for a moment to reflect on this and my mind wandered to naked lovers wearing Harvard sweaters and squealing like pigs as their bodies intertwined. The next thing I knew Guadalupe was prodding me by poking my knee with the pizza box.

"Mr. Zolly. Jou okay?"

"Uh, yeah, I'm great. I was just analyzing the evidence for a moment. So listen, you're saying you didn't hear anything unusual at all? I'm not necessarily talking about people moaning or groaning or anything like that, but just sounds."

"No, nothing unusual like that," she said after pausing in mid-bite to think.

"You see Guadalupe, a man was killed in 652 that Monday. He was shot. And you didn't hear any gunshots?"

"I swear I'm being honest with jou, I hear nothing."

"I believe you, but the police believe the murder took place someplace around the time you were working on the sixth floor. A couple people report hearing the gunshots and you didn't hear anything?"

"Jes that's right, but you see I was going up and down and up and down between floors five and six. Maybe I missed them. Or who knows, I may have had the water running to clean the bathtub or something."

"Sure."

"And even worse is the vacuum cleaner. Why in the name of Santa Maria do they have to be so loud? What good is a clean floor if you go deaf?"

She posed a puzzle I couldn't solve, so I moved on to my next question. "How about people? Did you see people coming in and out?"

"Jes. I think I did. I'm pretty sure. You know all these rooms look alike, and I was working hard, but sure I think so."

"Now this is very important. Did you see anyone you could identify coming out of room 652 that afternoon?"

"Jes. As a matter of fact now that you mention it jes, I remember somebody 'cause the way they were dressed. I mean maybe. I was keeping an eye open for my boss because I wasn't supposed to be there, I was working for my friend, my friend who had to go to the dentista, jou know? "

"Yes, she told me."

"Well I was watching for my boss, he's very tough and nobody likes him because he has a steak up his ass. I was watching for him just in the chance in a million he would actually know who I was and that I wasn't supposed to be there."

"Was this the person you saw coming out?" Excited that I might be onto something I showed her a publicity photo of a very angry looking J-Up. He was in his beret and leather vest and poking his hands at the camera in some sort of rapper sign language. He was either showing how bad he was or he had cramps in his fingers.

Guadalupe held the photo by its edge so as not to get any pizza sauce on it. She glanced at it for only a second before handing it back. "No. I don't see him. The person I see is a woman."

"A woman?" I said with surprise. So much for being onto something, Sherlock. "What did the woman look like? Can you describe her?"

"Jes, I was working on the sixth floor and when I come out to empty the trash in my cart, I hear a door opening down the hall. I turn and look and I see a none."

"Wait a second, I'm confused. You just said you saw a woman. Now you're saying you saw no one?"

"No, jou are not good listener. I say I saw 'none.'"

"Marone! I'm lost."

"A 'none,' como se dice, a sister from the church. You know?"

"Oh, a *nun.*"

"Isn't that what I say?"

"Well, yes and no, it's spelled different. One way it means 'no one or nothing,' another way it means 'a woman of the church.'"

"English is stupid to have one word means different things. What if 'up' means both 'up' and 'down?' You could fall on your ass listening to English."

"You're absolutely right, but let's move on from semantics, okay?"

"We can move from Sam whoever, I don't even know him."

"Fine. Now you said you saw a nun coming out of 652?"

"Not really a none," Guadalupe said, mulling it over in her mind as she took a swig of coke. "You see this woman she looked almost like a none. She had this long black scarf that wrapped all around her head and under her chin tight. It even wrapped over her forehead so all you could see below was her eyes." She used her hand to demonstrate and smudged her forehead with tomato sauce. "And I only see her eyes for a second because bam right away she puts on some big black sunglasses."

Holy crap! She had just described Ariélle's patented "I want to be alone" look. A little piece of cheese flew out of my mouth onto my lapel. Was this mystery woman Ariélle? Was she involved in murder?

"And this woman was coming out of 652?"

"Jes. I'm pretty sure. You see 652 is the last room at the end."

"Other than the way she was dressed, did you notice anything strange? Was she upset or running?"

"No, she walk normal. But she don't look very happy at all. Her face was all grime."

"Grime? Her face was... oh, you mean 'grim.' Like the grim reaper."

"Who's he? Is he related to this Sam Antic guy?"

"Never mind." I'd had enough running around in linguistic circles for one day. "Let me see if I've got this right." I showed her the picture of J-Up again. "You didn't see this man, but you saw the nun?"

"Jes."

"Okay. Is that all? Can you remember seeing anyone else coming out of 652?"

Guadalupe paused, either savoring the mozzarella or trying hard to remember. "No, I don't think so. I see a lot of people all day, but I remember this woman because she was dressed unusual like that."

"Okay, great. You're being a real big help here. But one more question, can you remember seeing this woman that day?" I took a photo of Sissy out of my blazer pocket and showed it to her.

"Oh jes, I know who she is, I see her all the time in the magazines and with her mother the famous singer when they stay in the hotel. Everyone says what a tacano the mother is."

"Excuse me, I don't know what that means. Tacano?"

"Let me think. It means... she cheeps."

"Cheeps? Like a baby chick?" Damn, we were back to animal sounds. Guadalupe looked very confused.

"She 'cheeps' like this?" I started cheeping and pecking like a chick. "Cheep, cheep, cheep..." Her look changed from confusion to "this hombre is loco," but I pressed on. "Are you saying she was like, an, umm, un pollo... un pollo baby?"

"No, no. 'Cheeps' like a cheeps skater. You'd think with all her money she'd be better, but no."

"Oh? Cheep*skate*, I get it. So did you this woman that day?"

"I see her all the time... Santa Rosa!" Suddenly a light bulb went off in Guadalupe's head. "Room 652! This is her room?! This is where the newspapers say she shoots her boyfriend?!"

"Yes, that's right. That's what they claim. But we don't know for sure. Did you see her Monday?"

"No Mister Zolly. I didn't even know she was on this floor. If I had seen this I would have told the police. Even if my boss with the steak up his ass fires me."

I wanted to make a crack about her boss' gourmet ass but knew better than to start down that path again, so I just thanked her for her help and reassured her no one was going to get fired.

"Thank jou Mr. Zolly, jou are a good man. And thank jou for an even better pizza. I'm around anytime jou want to feed me something."

"I just may take you up on that. If anything comes to mind about the day of the shooting, please give me a call."

I handed Guadalupe my business card and thanked her for the first-aid to my cat wounds. She looked at the card with trepidation, saying she didn't want to get anybody in trouble. I looked her in the eye and told her not to worry about that. You gotta tell the truth and let the chips fall where they may. I had to remind myself of the same thing. If the woman in the dark glasses and black scarf *was* Ariélle, and she was somehow involved in murder, I'd have to let her fall.

But how could Ariélle be a murderer? Not my dream girl! What possible motive could she have? Well off the top of my head I could come up with two - not a good sign. In the first Sissy shoots her fiancée and goes running to tell Mommy what she's done. As she had a thousand times in her life she pleads with her mother to make it right. Ariélle is in shock, but has the presence of mind to put on the scarf and glasses before leaving her room. Or maybe it's just force of habit. In either case Ariélle goes downstairs, sneaks into the murder scene and in a frantic attempt at a cover-up, wipes the gun clean of her daughter's fingerprints. If this is was what happened it all becomes a wasted effort after Sissy strolls into the cop house and confesses to murder.

The second scenario was far worse. Sissy runs from the room distraught over her boyfriend dumping or cheating on her and once again goes crying to Mommy. Ariélle, learning how Kyle hurt her baby, goes downstairs to confront him.

Somehow things get out of hand and she finds the gun in the nightstand and Kyle ends up getting shot. That's putting it nicely. What was more likely was an enraged Ariélle goes to the room carrying her gun with her. That would make it premeditated murder. But c'mon, was that possible? Ariélle a murderer? The woman has seven Grammy Awards for Christ's sake.

I sighed as I examined the facts. It's not that there weren't plenty of rumors about how Ariélle took care of the first cheating man in her life. Then there was the murder weapon. The gun was registered in Ariélle's name. And yeah, there was something else. Ariélle made a point of telling me how much trouble J-Up was, and that I should begin with him when looking for suspects. Was all that just to divert any suspicion from her, the real killer?

I didn't want to believe that. Besides, the mystery woman might not have even been Ariélle. The scarf and dark glasses could just be a coincidence. She might in fact be the "other woman" who was sneaking in for a tryst with Kyle while Sissy was supposed to be away. Maybe Sissy came back unexpectedly, walked in on them, and shot the cheating bum in a moment of blind anger. Of course why would Kyle risk banging his new girlfriend in his fiancée's bed? Or maybe that was the *very* reason. The danger. I knew from the strap-on discovery that I was dealing with some pretty kinky people here.

Whoa, wait a second, I was getting ahead of myself. This mystery woman might not even be connected to the murder. Guadalupe wasn't sure what time she saw her coming out of 652. It would sure help if Guadalupe could place her at the scene near the time old Kyle bought the farm. That would at least give the cops a second suspect.

As I left Guadalupe's apartment these thoughts were beginning to tie my stomach in knots and I popped a couple Maalox. The good news is I found my car unscathed and smiled a little as I climbed in behind the wheel of the Red Demon. "The Red Demon." That's the name I gave to my Mini-Cooper. What? You never named a car? Okay, let me re-phrase that – you never had a *girlfriend* who named a car and you had to start calling it that to keep things all cutesy and warm between the two of you? The stuff men do to get laid. It's damn embarrassing.

I took a deep breath. Hey, you could hardly smell cat piss. As I drove off I started to think that in a few days or weeks you'd never know some lucky-to-still-be-alive stray had used the floor as a litter box. I also started to think of guys I could call who would torch the Red Demon so I could collect the insurance money.

CHAPTER EIGHT

Traffic was bad and by the time I got back to Seaside I was running late. Did I mention I had a date? Keeping my pledge to Tina that we'd go out more we'd planned dinner at a fancy restaurant. My idea of fancy was anyplace that didn't use plastic forks, but Tina insisted on this great new place she'd found named "Tratatoria Fresca." Oh brother. Whenever you see the word "Tratatoria" it should be a warning to you to "trat" out of the joint in a hurry.

When I got to Tina's place she was already standing outside waiting and jumped in beside me in a rush. "Oh Zol, thank God you're here. I am starving baby."

"I'm sorry babe, traffic was bad."

"That's okay. Nothing is going to ruin this night." She leaned over to give me a kiss then suddenly put her hand over her stomach. "Oh wow, can you hear my stomach rumbling?"

"It's okay, we're not far. By the way, you look beautiful tonight." I slid my hand over hers on the seat.

"Thanks Zol, I... I..." Her voice trailed off as something unpleasant distracted her. She sniffed the air like a hound dog on the hunt. "Do you smell something Zolly?"

"Uh uh." I shook my head and acted like I was working hard to concentrate on the road.

Tina looked around to try and pinpoint what was bothering her. In a moment her eyes fixed on the rear-view mirror. "Why do you have three pine tree air fresheners?"

"They were on sale." Okay, maybe the cat piss was a tad more noticeable than I tried to convince myself. Thank you Mr. Fangs for the gift that keeps on giving.

"It smells like a litter box in here."

"Really? Why don't you try opening your window?"

"No the wind will ruin my hair," Tina declared as if reading some ancient stone tablet containing the immutable rules of womanhood. "Thou shall be overcome with asphyxiation before thou shall crack a car window and ruin thy hair."

"Baby, I..." she said, continuing her protest. Luckily she was interrupted by the ringing of my cell phone.

I flipped it open and wedged it under my chin. "Hello... Yes, this is Blaine Collins, who may I ask am I speaking to?" It was Catnip or J-Up or whatever his name was, taking the bait. "Oh, it's a pleasure to speak to you. I've been a fan a long time." If three seconds is a long time. "Listen, do you prefer 'J' or 'J-Up' or 'Jamie' or 'Mr. Upton? What do your friends call you?" There was a long silence on the other end of the line; maybe the guy didn't have any friends. Finally he muttered something like "Whatever, dude," and we moved on.

"That's right, three clubs spread from Cleveland to Zanesville. We like to call it the 'Entertainment Crescent of Ohio'... Yes, I'd like to sit down and discuss it... Of course I know how busy you are, but as a personal favor do you think we could meet sometime this week?" Oh brother. I was making myself sick. "Oh really. Dusseldorf? Tomorrow morning.... no I'd really rather not wait till you get back. Gee, I may have to give Helen Reddy a call, I hear she does a hell of a show from that wheelchair. What? Tonight?" Tina shook her head sternly and mouthed "No way!" Then she grabbed her belly and gave me a soulful look like kids in those ads asking you to feed the hungry.

"That would be great, where are you?" I said, giving her an "I'm sorry" glance.

With a resigned sigh Tina took a pen and paper out of her purse and handed it to me so I could scribble down the address. Holding a cell phone, scribbling and steering – I could do it all.

"Yeah, thanks, I'm looking forward to meeting you too," I said, hanging up on Mr. J-Up.

"How could you Zolly? I'm starving!"

"I know Hon, but this is gonna work out perfect. Would you believe that right now on this phone I was talking to none other than J-Up himself?"

Tina scrunched her eyes in confusion. "That singer guy?"

"Yeah, and he's invited us to come see his show tonight. Isn't that great? You're traveling in exclusive circles now babe."

"But Zolly I'm so hungry I'm gonna faint."

"Are you kidding? A classy joint like this guy plays has got to have awesome food. This is gonna be even better than we planned." I grinned at her and squeezed her knee on the seat beside me. Damn, I could feel her bones. "You gonna be okay Baby?"

"Yeah, sure," she said, always the trooper.

"Great, great, we'll be there in a flash, it's only in..." My eyes glanced down at the address scribbled on the paper. "Parsippany."

Marone.

If you don't know Jersey, Parsippany is at least a couple hours from Seaside, without traffic. "Without traffic." Don't you love when someone says that? When the hell *isn't* there traffic? It's like saying you could safely walk right into a nuclear reactor, "without radiation." I'm betting that on the first wagon trains crossing this great country some joker was sitting on a buckboard saying "We oughta be in Californy in six months, without Indians."

Tacked onto the two hour trip was another fifteen to twenty minutes to make rest stops on the Turnpike so Tina could use the facilities. God bless her, she's a great gal, but she's got the bladder of a hummingbird. I swear Tina doesn't even have to drink anything, just seeing condensation on the windshield is enough to make my honey have to pee.

So by the time we arrived in Parsippany poor Tina had bitten down all her fingernails and left gnaw marks on the dashboard. Or maybe those were from the cat. I also noticed later that one of the pine cone air fresheners was missing, but I'm not going to point fingers without proof.

J-Up. Parsippany. Yes sir, we had truly arrived. I pulled off Highway 46 into a parking lot and stopped the Red Demon so we could admire the magnificent building rising out of the expanse of asphalt before us: Snooky's Chateau Versailles. Magnificent. Banquet facilities like Snooky's Chateau Versailles were an invention of the late twentieth century New Jersey nouveau bourgeois. Before this period most people were content to hold their wedding reception at the V.F.W. or Knights of Columbus Hall. You got a good roast beef dinner cooked by elderly Polish or Sicilian ladies, and every table had as a centerpiece a bowl of kielbasa or Italian sausage that would be refilled until your belly ran out of room, and then some. But now that people had a little money they frowned on the blue-collar traditions of the peasants who spawned us, and in their unending quest to equal the French bourgeois constructed these banquet mega-plexes. A place like this could host three or more events at one time.

Located on the beautiful banks of the Jersey City Reservoir, between a discount tire warehouse and a Fish and Chips drive-through, the Chateau Versailles was a vision of Greek columns, Italian Marble, alabaster balustrades, and carved mahogany. It was a tantalizing glimpse of what Renaissance craftsmen might have achieved had they only been gifted with molded plastic.

The centerpiece of the palace was a grand two story entrance hall featuring a sweeping staircase where many a wedding party would pose for photographers. A cathedral ceiling above boasted a huge stained glass window resembling the one in the *Poseidon Adventure* that everybody falls through when the ship overturns. You had to wonder how many brand spanking new grooms had stared up at this window and felt that they too had lost their grip and were plunging to their deaths.

Outside the grand entrance hall was a courtyard graced with plastic topiary and highlighted by a multi-tiered faux marble fountain. Encircling the gently spouting water were life-size sculptures of wood nymphs, Greek maidens bearing water pitchers, and mob boss John Gotti. Okay, I'm kidding about the wood nymphs.

With a hunger weakened Tina hanging on my arm I entered the ornately carved wooden doors of the entrance hall and was immediately confronted with a problem. J-Up had told me where he was performing, but not at which of the three events being hosted that evening at the Chateau Versailles. While Tina went off on her unending quest for a ladies room, I checked out a black velvet directory listing the evening's events in movable plastic letters. The first was the DeMaggio's golden wedding anniversary. I immediately pictured a couple in their eighties with the wife yelling at her husband to turn up his hearing aid and his ignoring her on purpose as he had for decades. Somehow I didn't see them as fans of J-Up's music, even if they'd been able to hear it.

The next event was the Yoshizaki-Chandramouli wedding reception. Talk about your ethnic car crashes. Can you imagine if the wife was the liberated type who insisted on hyphenating their names? Yoshizaka-Chandramouli. Can you also imagine their poor kid in kindergarten? By the time he learned to write his name his peers would be celebrating their high school graduation. This party was a possibility, but I still didn't see a hall full of traditional Japanese and Hindu relatives being keen on boy bands. And to the best of my knowledge J-Up didn't play the sitar. So I moved on to the last listing: "The Saperstein Bar Mitzvah." Bingo! Teenage hormones, J-Up, it was a match made in schlub heaven.

But is this what it had come to? Poor J-Up was reduced to playing Bar Mitzvah's in the Jersey burbs? Well I guess you gotta do what you gotta do. And I guess it wasn't too horrible a gig for J-Up as long as no one spotted him stealing bottles of Seagram's from the open bar, and the dreamy eyed fourteen year old with an overbite didn't tell her parents how he tried to feel her up in the parking lot. Still I was beginning to feel sorry for the guy. Don't get me wrong, from the first time we met in the hotel corridor outside Sissy's room I thought he was an ass, but I was feeling the kind of sorry you feel for the bull in a bullfight.

With Tina back on my arm we proceeded to the banquet hall hosting the Saperstein party. I soon discovered this was one of those theme bar mitzvahs that had become so popular since we as a culture had collectively lost our minds and made Hollywood the be all and end all of our existence. The theme of this evening's festivities was "Star Wars." Guarding the entrance to the hall was an ice sculpture of Luke Skywalker under a banner that read "Mazel tov Kevin, May the Force be With You." At the foot of the statue was a Menorah made out of glowing light sabers.

"You brought me to a Bar Mitzvah, Zolly?" Tina asked incredulously. "This is the big night out you promised me?"

"Are you kidding baby? Didn't you read how bar mitzvahs are the trendiest thing going nowadays? There was a big piece about it in *People Magazine.* Bar mitzvahs are the new celebrity weddings."

"I must have missed that issue," Tina said, calling my bluff.

"Hey, J-Up is performing here, and he's a celebrity, sort of."

"You owe me, Zol," she said, not buying my b.s. for a second, but too weak to argue. "God you owe me so many I can't even remember what you owe me."

"Who's hungry?" I asked brightly. "I smell buffet!"

Trying to distract Tina by appealing to her hunger, I pulled her over to a buffet table containing huge bowls of shrimp prepared in every manner known to Jersey Man. Looking at them I was sure that the oceans had been denuded of shrimp and these were the last remaining on the planet.

The shrimp fest was book ended by carved watermelons. One was sculpted to represent a bust of Abraham, and its counterpart the face of Yoda.

But by far the crowning glory of the spread was a six foot long replica of Han Solo's Millennium Falcon molded out of chopped liver. It was obviously untouched and being preserved intact for photographs later, but before I knew what was happening the ravenous Tina had strafed a foot long section of its hull with a cracker. As an angry attendant approached I whisked Tina away and we disappeared in the crowd just as the lights dimmed and the ceremonies began.

Mr. Saperstein gave a moving speech about the pride and blessings his family felt on this joyous occasion. He then introduced his son Kevin Saperstein who wore thick black glasses and weighed in at sixty-five pounds dripping wet. Kevin thanked the crowd for coming, spoke about what the day meant to him, and concluded his remarks with "Today I Am a Jedi."

That was the cue for the entertainment to begin. Sparks cascaded from a cardboard model of an Imperial Star Destroyer as it jerked its way along a wire. Lights came up on a small raised stage revealing actors dressed as Moses and Princess Leia. A trio of Julliard trained musicians who must have been contemplating where their lives had gone wrong struck the Stars Wars theme. The Star Destroyer shot a pyrotechnic charge down another wire and exploded a paper mache planet earth. Princess Leia cowered under the arm of a wrathful Moses as he pointed his staff at the space ship and it in turn exploded into sparks.

J-Up, carrying a light saber and wearing a Darth Vader mask, bounded onto stage and burst into a song written especially for the evening:

"C'mon girl hit me with your death ray,
set that sexy phaser to stun.
My force is gonna be with you
before the night is done.
Oh yeah, oh yeah, oh yeah,
girl, girl, girl!"

Marone.

I was beginning to get that queasy feeling you get when you see a small animal run over on the highway. But to my surprise things only got worse. Moses, either wanting to ham it up, or himself having stolen some bottles of Seagram's; was dancing around J-Up and poking him with his staff. This was obviously meant to be J-Up's big solo number and he took offense at the improvisation. He began fending off the staff with his light saber and a sort of Cosmic/Biblical duel developed right before our eyes.

As the fight increased in intensity J-Up lunged for Moses, missed, and instead got his saber entangled in Princess Leia's long gossamer gown. In an attempt to free the saber J-Up ripped the skirt of the gown from Leia, exposing the purple thong she had so unwisely chosen to wear that evening. To the cheers of the men and the heart palpitations of the elderly women the mortified Princess fled the stage.

Moses and Darth Vader/J-Up abandoned their weapons and a shoving match developed, accompanied by some language not found in the Torah. Eventually J-Up proved the stronger or more sober and Moses went stumbling off the stage to the shrieks of the crowd. One aunt of advanced age screamed "He killed Moses!" before fainting. A loud chorus of boos slammed J-Up, and shouting something roughly translated as "go propagate yourselves" he stomped off the stage. All I know is if the real Moses had witnessed this he'd have lead his people back into the wilderness.

I turned to Tina with a weak smile. "Having fun?" She gave me a stare that could turn me into an ice sculpture. "I smell roast beef! Let me get you a sandwich." With that I snuck off toward the spot I'd seen J-Up/Vader disappear. "Doctor Harvey Florsheim," I barked waving my business card and threading my way through the crowd. "Does anyone require medical assistance?"

Through a service corridor and down a flight of stairs I found J-Up's dressing/storage room in the basement. I knocked on the door. I knocked harder. Finally a voice from inside answered: "I already cashed the check dude, get lost!"

"J-Up? It's Blaine Collins, from Collins Entertainment," I called through the door. I heard glass breaking and eventually a shell shocked J-Up opened the door. He wore a tee shirt that read "Victim" and was well on his way to becoming shit faced. Even if his eyes could focus I doubted he'd remember I was the dude he'd seen in the hall outside Sissy's room at the Babylon. I was betting at this point he wouldn't be able to recognize George Washington on a dollar bill. And I was right.

"Sorry about that Collins," he said, leaning precariously against the jamb. "I get so f-ing tired of everybody and their mother wanting f-ing autographs."

I looked around the empty corridor and didn't see a soul within miles, but didn't say anything except "Good show man."

"It would have been better dude if the band weren't so f-ing off key. I get so f-ing tired of working with amateurs, you know dude?"

I soon learned that J-Up's favorite word after "dude" was "f-ing." He used this shortened form of the f word after his publicist convinced him that the long form wasn't good for his image. J-Up respected her experience and wisdom. It didn't hurt that she was also f-ing him.

"Can I come in?" I asked.

"Oh yeah, sure dude," he answered, stepping aside and waving me into the small room. "Have a seat dude." I sat in a plastic folding chair beside a card table covered with makeup and liquor bottles. J-Up sat on a bale of paper napkins. "So about your clubs, I'd really like to play them dude, but I've got gigs way through New Year's."

"More bar mitzvahs?" I asked, unable to resist a little poke at his ego.

"No f-ing way dude. This gig tonight was a favor. No f-ing way they could pay what I get."

"Well I'm glad to hear you're doing so well and are all booked up, because I have a confession to make. My name isn't Collins and I don't own any clubs."

"Are you a cop man?!" He jumped off the napkins and his eyes opened and shut as they struggled to focus on me.

"No, I'm..."

"Because she swore she was f-ing 21," he sputtered, cutting me off.

"No, listen, I'm..."

"And if you're from the f-ing I.R.S. good luck dude, because all I have left is my toothbrush and the shirt on my back. You can take that if you want, sell it on f-ing E-bay or something."

"Look, my name is Zolly Michelangelo and I'm a private investigator," I finally was able to squeeze in between rants.

"You're not a cop?"

"No, I'm not." He studied me silently a long time, then asked nonchalantly:

"So dude, are you holding?"

"No, I'm not."

"Then why the hell are you wasting my f-ing time?" he said with a flash of rage. Yeah, like I was keeping him from his PhD. dissertation or his charity work in Africa.

"Dude it's time for you to join the f-ing others and go f-yourself." He used the long form of the word this time and showed me the door.

"This is important," I said, not giving ground. "I work for Ariélle. I'm investigating the murder of Kyle Broder."

"What the f- is there to investigate. The dude's still dead, ain't he?"

"Yes." My answer produced a big grin on J-Up's face.

"Investigation closed. See ya." He swung the door back and forth to prod my exit.

"Okay, I guess you don't really care what happens to Sissy. I guess you never really loved her." I started for the door. J-Up grabbed me by the shoulder and twirled me around.

"Don't you *ever* say that! Don't you *ever* say I don't love her dude! You don't know f-ing shit!"

"No? Then why don't you educate me"

"Yeah, that's what I should f-ing do. It's time for J-Up to tell his f-ing story. It's time for J-Up to..." He froze in mid thought and stared blankly at me, his jaw hanging open. I didn't know if he was thinking about something or his last brain cell had just died.

"You got something to say?" I asked. His tone suddenly became sorrowful; he sat in the folding chair and clasped his head in his hands.

"Nobody ever f-ing loved anybody like nobody knows like I f-ing loved Sissy. We were one person. It's like the girl's part of me, like my arm or foot or something, you f-ing know dude?"

I had no idea what the hell he was saying but nodded sympathetically. "Yeah, sure I do."

"I know all the jokes man. They say instead of J-Up my name oughta be F-up 'cause of the way I always screw everything up. But not this time. I love her dude. And I didn't screw it up. She dumped *me*! Can you f-ing believe it?!"

"Why do you think that is?" I put my hand on his shoulder sympathetically. Off the top of my head I could come up with a couple hundred reasons, but I wanted to hear what he thought.

"I don't go that way dude," J-Up said, pushing my hand off his shoulder. "I don't care about the f-ing rumors. That dude swore he was gonna put me in a Jackie Chan movie."

I rolled my eyes and took a step back. "Why do you think Sissy dumped you?"

"Because everybody uses J-Up, dude. I'm like the f-ing drive up window of the f-ing Bank of America. Drive right on up and make your f-ing withdrawal from my heart then drive right on out and leave me choking on your f-ing exhaust."

The dude was a real poet. I could see why his song lyrics were so deep and real. "That's beautiful, man." I had to fake a cough and cover my mouth to hide a laugh.

"Thanks dude, coming from a guy who owns his own f-ing clubs and all that shit, it means a lot to me."

I'm tired of saying "Marone" so you're going to have to imagine me saying it.

"Can you imagine she dumped J-Up, man? Nobody dumps J-Up unless they're..." He suddenly stopped himself and I filled in the rest of the sentence in my head: No one dumps J-Up: - unless they've got half a brain? – unless they've suddenly recovered their eye sight? – unless they've met him, - unless every other living invertebrate on the planet has suddenly gone extinct?

"Unless they're what?"

"No, no, no dude. I'm not talking, not yet." He laughed and leaned back against the door. "You work for f-ing Ariélle, that right dude?"

"That's right."

"Well why don't you go and f-ing tell her J-Up's tired of being f-ing used. It's his time to do the using. Yeah his turn."

"Just what do you mean by that?" My pupils constricted as I stared at him.

"Tell Ariélle it's time to take care of old J-Up, unless she wants the world to hear the truth about her precious f-ing Sissy."

I grabbed the punk and stuck my face in his. "What are you talking about, what do you know?" I growled.

"Hey, easy dude!"

"Oh, I'm sorry. But the only thing I hate more than washed up boy singers is washed up boy singers who make threats against my clients. And it sounded to me like you just made a threat against Ariélle."

"Who's making threats dude? All I'm saying is I think it's time Ariélle started showing me a little f-ing respect."

I let go of him and stepped back. "You know, I'm sorry, but that sounded like another threat. And since you like threats I've got one for you. How'd you like a permanent gig in Rahway State prison wearing a nifty new costume with a bulls eye over the butt?"

"What are you f-ing talking about dude?"

"I'm talking about you having the perfect motive to kill Kyle Broder. Everybody with a TV's heard you say if you can't have Sissy nobody can."

A big grin crossed his face. The kid actually seemed happy I thought he was capable of killing somebody. I guess it played up to the gangster image he had fabricated in his sick mind. He got cocky and started to bob his head as he talked.

"Yeah, well maybe I did cap the dude, or maybe somebody f-ing beat me to it. I've got a whole lot to say, and Ariélle better start listening."

So now he was into blackmail. I never advise my clients to go the blackmail route because it almost always turns out bad. But I wanted to feel the punk out and see what was going on in his delusional mind. "What do you want from Ariélle? You think she's going to give you money?"

"Dude, you're insulting me. J-Up's not about the money"

Yeah right, he's not about the money any more than a man with a plastic bag over his head is about the oxygen. "So this isn't about money?"

"F- no dude. This is about the music. About getting the music to my fans. You see dude, there's this conspiracy against J-Up. They like to build you up and then tear you down, you know?" I nodded as if he were making any more sense than a goldfish blowing bubbles. "Right now they're saying J-Up is over. They're trying to keep me from my fans and stop the music."

I'd support that. Show me a petition and I'll sign.

"But Ariélle knows the suits. She could put the word out that J-Up's cool. Hell, she might even use me as an opening act. Well not an opening act, we'd be like equals, but I'd go on first due to her being in the business a lot longer."

"So you're not looking for money?"

"Shit no." He paused. "But money would be cool too."

"I see where you're coming from dude," I said, trying not to gag.

"I'm only askin' what I deserve dude. It's time somebody started paying J-Up some respect."

I wanted to say "You could start by respecting yourself," but I was a private investigator, not a high school guidance counselor. I learned long ago that you're gonna meet a lot of messed up people in this line of work and you can't save them all.

J-Up must have sensed my pity because he gave me a forlorn look and spoke sincerely: "So dude, you sure you're not holding?"

I shook my head in disgust and walked out. As I made my way back to the banquet hall I tried to wrap my mind around what I had just learned. J-Up was what we in the business technically call "an ass." He was an empty vessel who changed personalities like he changed hats. All talk and zero substance. I doubted he could "cap" a tube of toothpaste. Still, love does crazy things to people.

And if that was the case I was back to my old problem. If J-Up had killed Kyle, why would Sissy confess to it? What reason on earth could she have to cover for that idiot? Did she felt guilty for dumping him? Maybe it was like dropping a dog off at the S.P.C.A. Even though he ate half your shoes and bit the mailman you still feel a little regret. But enough to take a murder rap for him?

When I got back to the hall I found Tina dancing the Horah with Moses. A photographer who seemed to be taken with her was snapping pictures like it was a fashion shoot. I chuckled as I imagined the bar mitzvah boy twenty years from now wondering who the hell the hot chick was.

Moses also seemed more than a little taken with Tina. He had apparently recovered from his fall off the stage and was feeling a tad too frisky for my comfort. His arm was draped around Tina's neck and his hand rested enthusiastically on her ass as they bounced to the beat of a klezmer band. From the look of things good old Moses had intentions of parting my girlfriend.

I remedied the situation by whispering in his ear that a plague was about to strike a part of his anatomy that would preclude him from ever having "first born." I then took Tina by the hand and led her toward the exit. The poor kid was so weak she had to lean against me to remain standing.

"I'm not feeling so good Zol," she said woozily. And on the drive home Tina and my Red Demon learned the perils of ingesting gefilte fish and Mai Tai's on an empty stomach. Well at least the car didn't smell of cat piss anymore.

CHAPTER NINE

I had to talk to Ariélle but of course to talk to her I had to go through Tammara the pit bull. She wanted to know everything I'd learned in my investigation so far: who I'd talked to, when, what they said, whether I believed them; and what conclusions I'd drawn if any. I began to wonder if her time in the army was spent working as a prison interrogator. It was all very cordial and polite mind you, but by time I was done I felt like I'd been water boarded with Chanel No. 5.

I tried to be cordial even though I was tempted to tell her to go propagate herself. But I realized I was dealing with celebrities and they live in a whole different dimension. Plus it was their dime so I'd put up with the b.s. - to a point. When I told Tammara I needed to talk to Ariélle personally, she insisted I tell her, Tammara, whatever it was and she would pass it on. When I refused the pit bull relented but still wanted to know the subject of my proposed conversation. I told her that I had dug up strong evidence that her personal assistant, a Miss Tammara King, was actually an alien from the planet Zircon.

The phone went silent for a few minutes while I'm guessing Tammara either spoke to her boss or put a contract out on my head. When she returned, slightly less cordial now, she set up a time for me to meet with Ariélle.

I arrived at Ariélle's suite in the Babylon a couple of hours later carrying a chunk of red meat as a peace offering for Tammara. Actually I had thought of bringing red meat but after a lot of debate settled on some Johnson's World Famous saltwater taffy. It wasn't necessary because Tammara was all cordial again and acted like nothing had happened. She led me into the same dark room where I had first met Ariélle. Only this time we weren't alone. Marshall was doing some strange shit involving strands of Ariélle's hair and strips of aluminum foil. It was either a hair treatment or they were making their own set of rabbit ears for the TV. A young Cambodian woman named Lai Duong was finishing Ariélle's pedicure.

Ariélle sat on the sofa reading *Vanity Fair* with her feet propped up on a small ottoman. I had never seen her bare feet before and felt humbled that Ariélle was relaxed enough around me to include me in her inner circle: hair stylist, pedicurist, and private investigator.

Without making it look obvious I snuck peeks at Ariélle's naked, milky white feet out of the corner of my eye as Lai pampered them like precious objects. To be honest I'd always thought that guys with foot fetishes were a little sick, but when I saw Lai masterfully painting an exquisite nail a vivid blushing pink – I was moved. Judge not lest ye be judged someone once said. I think it was one of those TV judges.

In a moment Ariélle dismissed her entourage so that we could speak privately. Tammara stayed behind until I objected strongly enough that Ariélle asked her to leave. From the scowl on Tammara's face I was sure that I wouldn't be able to make my way out of the suite past her without sustaining multiple teeth marks on my shins and ankles.

Once alone I told Ariélle about my meeting with J-Up and the demands he was making. She sat motionless as I spoke, her eyes as big and dark as in those drawings of aliens made by people claiming to have been abducted. I was abducted myself, hypnotized by her serene beauty.

I finished my little spiel by telling her that what J-Up wanted was blackmail pure and simple; and that in my experience I'd never seen a case where giving in to demands from scum like him had ended well.

Ariélle stared out the window at the ocean beyond for several long moments during which I couldn't even detect a blink of her eyes. Then she turned to me and said: "I don't zee what choice I have Zahlee." She had made up her mind. She needed to hear what J-Up had to say about Sissy. What would happen if J-Up revealed something that strengthened the cops' case against her? No, she had to find out what he knew. And what could it cost her? Money? She was already about to lose her daughter, what could be worse than that?

It was at that moment I witnessed for myself that it was more than beauty and a voice that had sustained Ariélle's long career. Once she made her decision her keen business mind raced to formulate a plan. Before I even had the chance to object she was on the phone to Tammara, asking her to obtain ten thousand dollars in cash for Zahlee. "Obtain." These people talked about putting their hands on ten grand like it was ordering a pizza.

Ariélle's plan was for me to meet with J-Up again. I wouldn't offer him any money at first. Instead I'd offer him Ariélle's help to get him into a good rehab program. Then I'd promise if he cleaned up she'd put him in touch with her agent and publicity people and they'd engineer a campaign to re-launch his career. The media love a good come-back story. They love tearing someone down and then accepting him back after he's repented and groveled at their feet.

If J-Up agreed to her plan Ariélle would meet with him personally. This would be a meeting to get the ball rolling on his new life, and a chance for the very persuasive Ariélle to dig out whatever dirt he might have on Sissy. If he didn't agree to this fresh start, then, well, I would have a briefcase full of cash in my car to buy his silence.

"Will you do thees for me Zahlee?" Ariélle asked soulfully, the dark oceans of her eyes washing over me in warm waves, her ivory feet seducing each other on the ottoman as she shifted.

Was there ever any question?

I tried calling J-Up's cell phone a few times but he was
either too high to hear it ringing or just ignoring anybody
but his dealer. Finally he called me one night about three in
the morning. When I asked him if he knew what time it was
the closest he could get to an answer was "August." I told him
that Ariélle had agreed to meet with him, but that he'd have
to meet with me first to set the ground rules. He balked at
the idea, saying his Porsche was in the shop and it was a bitch
getting around, but I insisted that this was a take-it-or-leave-
it proposition. "Then f-ing leave it dude!" he screamed into
the phone, deciding to call my bluff. "And you can leave that
f-ing Sissy to rot in some shithouse jail for the rest of her life
for all I care!"

After managing to calm him down I proposed that he
didn't have to have a car, that I would come to him. Judging
from his earlier flash of anger he was in a bad way and in
need of some quick cash to feed his habit; so I held my
ground and he finally relented. When I asked him where he
wanted to meet I heard him put down the phone and talk to
someone in the room. A young female voice answered in the
background and J-Up cursed in surprise, asking "how the f-
did I get here?!"

The girl's voice was soft and nervous, and I could make
out that she was worried about her parents catching her. But
J-Up asked when they were coming back and told her it was
cool because he'd be gone by the weekend. The girl continued
to fret but J-up slipped into his best hurt puppy voice and

asked "don't you love me baby?" There was silence as the girl weighed her love for him with the fear her parents would walk in and discover her in "mid-love."

I couldn't believe what I heard next. J-Up, his voice coarsened by whiskey and exhaustion, began to sing to her. The song talked about "my true booty love," but at that point I turned on the TV and found something more interesting to listen to - a documentary about dust mites.

After what seemed an eternity – the equivalent of fifteen seconds of a J-Up serenade – he got back on the phone. Now he was as euphoric as his mood was dark just minutes ago. He gave me an address and I scribbled it down on my official private investigator's note pad – a Milky Way wrapper. We agreed on a time but before I could hang up J-Up said he wanted me to know something. He was worried I was getting the wrong idea about him. He would never do anything to hurt Sissy. But his back was up against the wall and a dude had to do what a dude had to do. Besides, Ariélle was sitting on piles of cash as high as... as high as ... a high thing, you know, and the chick wouldn't miss any.

I pointed out that blackmail was one of the things that might give people the wrong impression about ole J-Up.

He said he knew he was "J-Up the Screw Up" and just wanted a second chance. Then he made me promise to give a message to Sissy. As he spoke I wrote his words down with my special pen that writes on thin air. He wanted me to tell Sissy he still loved her, and he forgave her for getting engaged to that other dude. He went on to say he loved her another five times, and that he'd take her back anytime she realized she was acting like a f-ing bitch.

It wasn't exactly a Shakespeare Sonnet, but I told him I'd pass on the sentiment. After agreeing on a meet time I hung up and tried to get some sleep. I spent the rest of the night pitching back and forth in my bed, wracked by a nightmare in which I was running away from J-Up as he tried to serenade me. I finally found myself atop a mountain of dollar bills, with J-Up backing me up to the precipice. I saw I was trapped, and as he started to close in I pulled out a gun and shot him in the heart. His lifeless body fell into my arms, but at the last moment turned into a giant Milky Way bar. So maybe it wasn't a nightmare after all.

The next afternoon I used MapQuest to locate the address J-Up had given me. I then met with Tammara King and told her I was headed to Hammonton, a small suburb not far from Atlantic City. After a bureaucratic grilling requiring everything from the exact address, J-Up's phone number, my mother's maiden name, and a blood test, Tammara issued me an attaché case containing ten grand.

"Pleasant" is a good word to describe Hammonton. I found myself parked in front of the very pleasant lawn of a very pleasant split-level house on a very pleasant cul-de-sac. There was a pleasant plastic windmill in the pleasant flower bed.

It hardly seemed the kind of place you'd find a hip gangsta like J-Up, but I remembered Sissy saying J-Up's address was usually the bed of a groupie from his last show. Putting this together with the conversation I overheard on the phone between J-Up and the young female worried about her parents, I concluded that this was probably exactly what happened. A dreamy eyed young fan crossed paths with the boy singer she idolized, she happened to mention her parents were out of town, and bingo she had herself a roommate. But the young girl had good reason to be worried. If her parents found her in bed with a twenty-six year old alcoholic/druggie that wouldn't be "pleasant."

I sighed, dreading the prospect of the parents returning while I was there. It might be tough to explain to the cops what I was doing in an underage kid's bedroom with a drug addict and a briefcase stuffed with ten grand. Can you say "dealer?" All I wanted to do was deliver Ariélle's message to the punk and get the hell out. As I glanced up at the house to make sure I had the right number, some movement behind the drapes in the big picture window caught my eye. I thought I saw a face peeking out at me. And then it was gone.

"Okay, here I go," I said, dragging my ass out of the Red Demon. As I made my way up the sidewalk I looked around and didn't see any activity on the entire block except for a portable lawn sprinkler a couple doors down. The thing jerked around in a circle making a hissing sound. Okay, I deserved to be hissed at. This wasn't my favorite part of the job.

Bang! Suddenly I heard a loud thump and a whoosh of air. My eyes snapped to the front door of the split-level as a young girl slammed through the heavy aluminum storm door onto the porch. Thin and fragile, her bones strained against the taut skin covering them, turning the flesh white. And there was a lot of flesh to see. She was naked except for a pair of baby blue panties and a pink crocheted comforter that her shaking hands clutched to her chest in a futile attempt at modesty.

Her reddened panicked eyes locked on mine in a stare that blended fear and sickening dread. Her trembling lips tried to form words but nothing came out but a thin line of drool that ran down her chin.

"Do you need help?" was the first stupid thing I could think to say. Her body shuddered and her eyes rolled white as she took off running across the lawn without answering. "Wait!" I called after her. But she continued her sprint, her long thin legs loping like a gazelle pursued by a lion. She gave an anguished scream and arched her back as the cold spit of the lawn sprinkler splattered her body, then she disappeared down the block. A dread of my own filled my belly as I started to wonder what the former boy band singer had done to drive the girl out of the house. The possibilities were endless.

Sucking it up, I climbed the steps to the porch and opened the aluminum storm door. The heavy wooden door inside was still open wide from the girl's hurried exit. I knocked on it and called out, but no one answered; so I did the only polite thing, I walked in. I took a few steps into what was a living room and called out again but the only sound I heard was some music playing in another part of the house.

Now let me give you a tip. If you ever want to learn a little about the people living in a house, just take a look at the mantle over the fireplace. Luckily these people had one and it was covered with the usual array of family photographs capturing cherished moments. On the far left was a silver framed photo of a pleasant looking young bride and groom on their wedding day. Her eyes stared off into the future, at the same time the wide lapels of his tux grounded them in the seventies. Next to it was a photo of the same couple grinning broadly as they held an infant they must have just brought home from the hospital. Moving on in perfect chronological order the infant grew into a little girl right in front of my eyes. Here she was almost too young to sit up but valiantly riding a pony. There she was a little older, standing in front of the Disneyland sign and wearing a pair of mouse ears. Next she posed proudly in a dance leotard and beret before a backdrop of the Eifel Tower. And before you knew it she was blowing out candles on a birthday cake celebrating "sweet sixteen." Sweet alright. The same sweet I'd seen running half naked down the block. Brother. Plant a radish get a skunk weed. You wonder what went wrong and if it could have been avoided.

So here I was in this pleasant living room in this pleasant house in this pleasant neighborhood hoping I wouldn't find anything unpleasant but having a feeling in my gut I would. I tilted my head to listen to the music again and realized that it was a CD of my favorite boy singer – J-Up himself. Besides becoming familiar with his voice I was tipped off by the fact the song lyric consisted mainly of the word "girl" repeated about seven hundred times.

I followed the music up a half-flight of stairs to the bedroom level. It was coming from a room at the end of the hall that was decorated by a teenage girl at the zenith of sweetness. My keen investigative instincts told me her name was "Jennifer," probably because "Jen's Room" was spelled out on the door in big glittery letters. Below were a multitude of photos cut out of magazines featuring pandas and unicorns and puppies at the pinnacle of their sweetness. Everyone was feeling sweet – except for me. The smell of ozone was prickling the hairs in my nostrils.

I called out again for propriety's sake and was met by the CD switching to a track featuring a song that began with the word – you guessed it – "girl." My hand accidentally poked the eye of a unicorn as I pushed through the door and stepped in.

Inside I found myself in a shrine. The room was a veritable Sistine Chapel of teen-dom, its walls and ceiling papered with

photos of teen hunks from *Tiger Beat* and *Bop Magazines*. On
the floor was a boom box playing the music that had lured
me. In the center of the shrine, lying on a funeral pyre of
pink taffeta and satin sheets was the body of a young man.
Dressed only in briefs, his torso was twisted convulsively and
his legs splayed as if fleeing some torment. By some cruel joke
of fate his face jutted toward the ceiling and his eyes frozen
wide stared up at a poster of a boy band. A band featuring a
kid who in his fifteen minutes of fame was known as "J-Up."

Later the girl I'd seen running semi-nude from the house
would be found hiding at a friend's house down the block.
She'd tell the police how she'd awakened after a "nap" feeling
cold, and discovered in horror the cold was coming from
contact with the body in bed next to her. After calming her
hysteria the friend's mother would convince her she had
to face her parents, that there was nothing that couldn't be
forgiven. Thinking back on the time when Slowicki's wife
died, I somehow found comfort in those words and could
only hope they were true.

Jennifer would tell the police how J-Up had been staying
with her while her parents vacationed in Hawaii. She'd
relate how that morning J-Up had been in a dark mood that
deepened when he got a call on his cell. She heard him get
into a heated argument that had him screaming at the person
on the other end. He must have won the argument and gotten
what he wanted because by time the conversation ended he
was elated.

Jen reluctantly loaned him the family car and together the two drove to a seedy neighborhood in Atlantic City. The girl was scared to stay alone but J-Up made her remain in the car while he went off to take care of some business. An hour later she was beginning to panic and wanted to flee but was afraid to leave the safety of the car. Ironically she was old enough to have a lover but still too young to have a driver's license. When J-Up jumped back in the car he was flush with excitement and drummed the dashboard with his hands while singing one of his band's old hits. J-Up was finally getting what he deserved and it was party time! The two drove to Jen's house to celebrate, but it wasn't much fun for Jen since there was still a trace of "sweet" in her that didn't allow experimenting with hard drugs. And soon after shooting up J-Up became almost comatose and didn't add much to the party.

The cops would find a paper bag with several thousand dollars in cash in a drawer near J-Up's body. There was also a stash of unusually pure heroin that the coroner would later determine contributed to his over dose. "Death by purity," it was another irony in a day full of ironies.

This was one of those times you have to step back and take a fresh look at things. My gut was telling me that J-Up's death wasn't an accident. Was it possible he just happened to lay his hands on the cash and drugs at the same time he'd cooked up his little blackmail scheme? Maybe, but in my business I've come to believe there aren't any coincidences. Whenever you come across what appears to be a coincidence it's a good thing because if you pick at it long enough you'll usually have your worst suspicions confirmed. And right now my suspicion was that somebody wanted to shut the boy band singer up. Either the drugs were a payment to buy his silence, or the giver knew about their purity and the likelihood of an over dose that would ensure his silence. Unfortunately when you made a list of people who had motive for either, Ariélle was right at the top.

Yeah, I had to step back and realize the people I was dealing with may not have been what they seemed. Had I allowed Ariélle's celebrity and my adolescent crush on her to color my judgment? Like most people finding themselves in the presence of celebrity I may have been taken in by the public image and made the mistake of believing I really knew the woman. I had to admit to myself now that it was entirely possible Ariélle was capable of murder.

CHAPTER TEN

If I were a betting man, and I am, I would have given odds a misguided J-Up killed Kyle Broder for taking Sissy away from him. Whether he was high and got carried away in a moment of jealous passion or his limited mind had premeditated it, it didn't make all that much difference to Kyle. Dead was dead.

But all bets were off now. With J-Up out of the picture I was back to square one. So I decided that instead of going from killer to victim it was time to start with the victim and figure out who might want him dead. Since I'd only met Kyle in death on a slab in the morgue, it was a good time to find out what people knew and thought about the guy in life. I started where he worked – the gym.

The gym owner was an ex-prize fighter named Dandy Duggan who apparently was a contender to be a contender back in the fifties. I expected to find him holed up in a dark seedy gym littered with punch drunk has-beens and old jock straps – a place right out of some old black and white boxing movie. Only in the movies you didn't have to smell the place.

I was surprised to find "Dandy's Gym" an antiseptic chrome and glass building anchoring a modern strip mall

in the Atlantic City suburbs. Inside health worshipers were
sprinting on treadmills like crazed hamsters in a wheel, giving
the place the appearance of a giant Habitrail. It's ironic that
our parents and grandparents slaved away in sweat shops to
give us a better life, and we choose to spend that life making
ourselves sweat. But don't get me started.

Inside I walked to a reception counter manned by two
twig-like young women wearing tight tee shirts with "Dandy"
emblazoned across the breast. Not a bad advertisement. They
were deep in discussion about quantum physics, or maybe
American Idol, with a fit young man who wore gym shorts
and had teeth brighter than a light house. Now I hate to
judge people based on first impressions, but trust me, the
three of them working together couldn't find their finger on a
map.

And a strange thing happened. Somewhere between the
parking lot and the counter I must have become invisible
because I stood in eye range a good five minutes without any
of them acknowledging my presence. If I were here to buy a
membership I'd have turned around and left before daring
to interrupt their important conversation. God knows how
much business they'd lost. But maybe I'm being too hard on
them. Maybe I don't look like a guy who needs a gym. Maybe
I'm perfect already.

Finally I started to cough like I was gonna spit up a turkey
and their eyes turned on me like they'd spotted a roach. They
got worried looks on their faces that I might be contagious,

and drawing mental straws quickly pushed forward the twig who I'm guessing was the receptionist. She had short black hair with wide green and red streaks and I instantly nick-named her "Christmas."

I asked Christmas if she knew Kyle and she told me right off, without having to check her Blackberry that she worked with him here at the gym for a couple years. I asked if she could tell me anything about the guy and after a lot of thought and what I think was a puff of smoke from her left ear, she announced: "Oh yeah, he's dead." I stepped back and my eyes widened in my best "I'm shocked" look. I asked "how?" and "why?" and Christmas replied with the in-depth kinda answer that would have earned her a minus 200 on her SAT's if she hadn't overslept that day. "Got killed," was the most complex sentence she could form. I asked if she knew anything else about the guy: who he was dating, who his favorite American Idol was, stuff like that. Christmas suddenly got suspicious or bored and said she didn't really know Kyle at all.

I told her that was too bad, because I had met Kyle and was thinking of buying one of those lifetime memberships. Maybe she could help me. Ding! Ding! Ding! The idea of scoring that fat commission caused Christmas's eyes to roll in her head like the spinning barrels on a slot machine. I could actually see pots of gold appear on her pupils. Along with images of all the cool clothes she was about to buy. What do you know, we suddenly became bosom buddies.

As Christmas went into her spiel about the benefits of gym membership, and the super plans Dandy's offered, I managed to sneak in a few questions. Like did she know if Kyle had been "friendly" with any of his clients or maybe was involved with one of the girls working at the gym. Christmas said no, but it wasn't for lack of effort on the part of the girls. After all, the guy was a stud and a really good dresser. He just never seemed interested and always had the same stock answer: "I'm seeing somebody."

"His fiancée, Sissy Strasbourg."

"Yeah, if that's what you want to believe."

"You don't?"

"Well he never talked about her, never brought her around. If you were dating a big celebrity wouldn't you want to rub other people's noses in it? I know I would."

"Who wouldn't?" I shrugged.

"Plus, more than once," she continued, pressing her palm over my hand on the counter, "And I'm only telling you this because you're a good friend... More than once Sissy called here when Kyle told her he was working – and he wasn't. You know what that's all about." She dipped her chin and gave me a knowing look.

I thanked Christmas for her help and asked if I could speak to her boss. But she wasn't about to let go of her pot of gold. Like an octopus wrapping her tentacles around me she started a sales spiel about how this was the very best time to join the very best gym in Atlantic City. I finally broke loose by giving her my phone number and promising I only wanted to check out the gym's owner - that any membership I bought would be from her.

Christmas glowed with visions of Dolce and Gabbana shoes dancing in her head as she picked up a phone and called her boss. Then she personally escorted me, arm around my shoulder, to a stainless steel staircase leading up to offices on a second story balcony lining the gym.

"Michael, good to see you," Dandy said, getting up from behind his teak desk. He had a mane of shocking white hair as thick as a lion's and a chest like a brick wall.

"Uh, no, the name's not 'Michael.'"

"Oh? I thought the girl said you were Michael Angelo!" His laugh exploded like a bazooka. "Do you think I could commission you to paint my kitchen?" My eardrums split again. I could have told him how un-clever I found that joke the first twenty-two thousand times I'd heard it, but instead I extended my hand.

"Call me Zolly."

"Zolly, look at me, would you believe I'm 92 years old?!"

"You're 92?!"

"No, I'm 72!" He let out another sonic boom and the windows rattled. "But punch my stomach, go ahead, punch it."

"Mr. Duggan, I..."

He interrupted me by flexing his bicep. "Go ahead, punch my arm, I'm old enough to be your grandfather and I won't even feel it."

"Mr. Duggan, as interesting a proposition as that is, I didn't come here to punch any part of you."

"Zolly, I could strip you down to fighting weight in three months!"

"Well, that would be excellent if I was planning to fight anybody, but I'm not. Besides, I'm only a few pounds heavier than when I was in high school."

"So you had a weight problem even then?" he said, giving me a sympathetic frown. "Don't be ashamed, that doesn't mean you're a lazy bum who disrespects his body, with some people it's genetic."

I was beginning to feel like maybe I *would* like to get into fighting shape so I could go a few rounds with him right then. But instead I told Dandy I was investigating the Kyle Broder murder and asked if he could tell me anything about his former employee.

"Eh, Kyle was a decent guy." I could tell he was choosing his words carefully.

"I see. Did he ever have problems with anybody here? An argument, something that might have caused a grudge?"

"Nah, Kyle got along okay with everybody." There was a tone to his voice that told me this wasn't exactly a ringing endorsement.

"But?" I asked. He hesitated and looked at me sheepishly. I could tell he wasn't the kind of man who liked to speak poorly of the dead. After debating a minute he cocked his head.

"It was none of my business, but Kyle was one of those guys who skate through life. I mean, he was a good trainer, and personable, but he never wanted to work hard enough to take it to the next level."

"How so?"

"When I upgraded to this new facility three years ago I made Kyle an offer to come in as a quarter partner, be the good looking front man to bring in the young crowd. But he wasn't interested. To tell the truth a guy with his looks and charm ought to have his own gym by now. But kids today, nobody thinks about the future. They earn a buck they spend a buck."

"So Kyle wasn't good with money?"

"Oh, he must have been doing something right lately. You'd never catch him out of one of those Italian suits that go for two grand. To think in my day you could have bought a house for that!"

"So he liked expensive clothes."

"And cars. He drove around in one of those fancy BM's."

Wha? I thought. "Oh, you mean "BM-W's?" "Yeah. Tiny two seat piece of crap that cost more than a Caddy. Can you believe that? Maybe he had a rich daddy or something, 'cause he was blowing dough like there's no tomorrow. Kids!" He punctuated his disdain with a disapproving "puh!"

"Maybe he didn't have a rich daddy, but he had a rich girlfriend," I said, not realizing it was out loud.

"Yeah, that Sissy, the one who got all famous for eating a bug. I seen her."

"I guess Kyle introduced you."

"Nah, I know her from the pictures in the paper. She never stepped foot in here, maybe we weren't high class enough..." His sentence trailed off and his eyes got that look like he was someplace else. "Hey," he said finally, tilting his head like he was curious about something.

"What?"

"You talking about that dame coming around has got me thinking."

"Oh, so you did meet her?"

"Nope, I'm thinking about the one who *was* here. When I told you I never saw Kyle argue with anybody, I forgot her. A couple weeks ago this doll stomps in and goes right over to Kyle while he's spotting a client on the weight bench. She starts getting loud and Kyle hurries her out into the parking lot. I couldn't make out what they were saying, but by the way her arms were slicing the air I could tell it was pretty nasty."

"Was this the woman?" I took out a photo of Sissy.

"No, that's Sissy. I'm not talking about her."

"Well what did the other woman look like?"

"I guess you could say she was average."

Average? Jeez Marie, I was dealing with a real Sherlock Holmes here. "Did she have hair, eyes? Did they have a color?"

"She was too far away to make out the color of her eyes. But her hair was black, or dark brown."

"Is there anything else you can tell me about her?"

"Only that she was 'average.'"

"Average? Well that gives me something to go on. Thanks for your time." I always try to be polite despite my urge to bludgeon somebody. I handed him my business card. "Give me a call if you think of something, okay?"

Duggan nodded, and then seemed to get an idea. "Hey, there is something."

"What" I asked hopefully.

"We're running a 'pay for three months get six' special. Sign up and I personally guarantee you'll lose that gut."

Gut? I sucked in hard and looked down to assess the situation. What, I was maybe two, ten pounds overweight? That's in the margin of error.

"Hey, I got a better proposal. How about you pay me for six and I never show up?"

Duggan stared at me a few moments before realizing it was a joke. "You're a real comedian," he said with a roar that almost knocked the fedora off my head.

"I promise to give it some thought," I said. And I did, for about three seconds before I started to give some thought to the pork roll sandwich I was gonna have for lunch. Should I have fries or potato salad with it? Hmm.

CHAPTER ELEVEN

Back on the Parkway traffic was murder. Besides the usual beach traffic the right lane was blocked by a bus that blew a tire. It was one of the thousand buses a day carrying senior citizen groups from New York and northern Jersey down to Atlantic City. Cattle car after cattle car of golden-agers would be dumped off at a casino for the day, fed a buffet lunch and fleeced of their social security checks at the slot machines. Now look, I got nothing against senior citizens, or gambling for that matter. But with everyone crying and hollering about social security going bust was it a good idea to rob these people out of hundreds of millions of dollars a year?

At the very least, wouldn't it be smarter if the *government* owned the casinos? Then at least the money they took off the old folks could be recycled back into the social security fund. How come everybody seems to have good ideas except the politicians? But don't get me started.

A group of about fifty seniors who had filed off the disabled bus were standing on the shoulder of the road and milling around in confusion, much like the scene when a truck load of chickens overturns and the cages break open.

Heads bobbed and eyes widened as they gawked at the wounded bus and the rows of backed up cars. One eager old broad in a straw hat tied with a purple scarf was having an animated discussion with the bus driver. With my window rolled down I swear I heard her ask where the buffet was. Another old guy had wandered to the rear of the bus and was trying to put quarters in the exhaust pipe. God bless 'em. Was this the great reward awaiting me after a lifetime of hard work and walking the straight and narrow?

Not going anywhere fast, my mind drifted back to the facts of my case. According to the hotel maid, Guadalupe, she saw a mystery woman in dark glasses and a scarf leaving the murder scene. And then there was the woman Dandy Duggan told me came to the gym and argued with Kyle. Another mystery woman, or could it be the same one?

Was she Kyle's new girlfriend and did Sissy walk in on them and fly into a murderous rage? If so, and the mystery woman had seen Sissy plug her man, wouldn't she have come running down the hotel corridor screaming for help? Guadalupe said she was walking calmly. Maybe because this mystery woman had nothing to do with the murder. Guadalupe couldn't even remember if she'd seen her before or after Kyle bought it. But if she *was* there at the time of the crime, was she walking calmly because she was a cool customer and too smart to call attention to herself? Was *she* the one who pulled the trigger?! Yeah, maybe she was an *old* girlfriend not willing to part with Kyle, or maybe she was the new girlfriend all pissed off because Kyle wouldn't leave Sissy. And why would he, she was the gravy train supplying him with designer suits and BM's. I mean BMW's. Was Kyle's plan for an even bigger jackpot marrying into Ariélle's money brought to a sudden end by this vengeful other woman?

Wait a minute. If Sissy saw this mystery woman shoot her fiancée why would Sissy confess to the crime? Damn. It always came back to that. The best explanation was the simplest, and the one Sissy had already told the cops. For whatever reason, Sissy was the one who shot Kyle. Who else would have known there was a gun stashed in the nightstand drawer? If... if in fact that's where the gun came from. Wait a minute. I was assuming Sissy was telling me the truth about the gun being in the nightstand. She or someone else could have brought it with them. I was breaking one of my cardinal rules. Never assume anything.

The gun. The gun. *A* gun? If there were two women in that room, Sissy and the mystery woman, why was I assuming there was only one gun? My hand darted to my cell phone inside my blazer and I speed dialed Slowicki's direct number.

"Detective Slowicki," the voice answered. It was either a voice or somebody was sandpapering a moose.

"Slowicki, it's me," I said impatiently.

"Oh, Zolly, I was just about to call you. I got some real important news."

"About my case?"

"About you. I heard there's a new clothing store at the mall called 'Pygmies 'R Us.'" At that point I heard something erupt out of his nose. I could only hope it was his beverage.

"Funny. You know with your sense of humor and people skills, you ought to audition for that TV Survivor Show."

"You think they'd take me as a contestant?" Slowicki asked.

"No, but I hear they're looking for an island."

After the pleasantries concluded I asked Slowicki if he was sure the cops had found only one gun at the murder scene. Slowicki browsed through his file with the speed of a chariot race – a chariot race where the horses had been replaced by snails. At one point I swore I heard snoring, but it might just have been his emphysema. "C'mon, I yelled into the phone, I only got three million minutes a month on my calling plan." Finally he got back on the phone and re-confirmed that only one gun had been found.

I was disappointed, but the two women in the room theory kept running through my head and led to another inspiration. I asked if the forensic report was certain that all the bullets fired in the hotel room, especially those finding unlucky Kyle's body, were from the same gun. Another pause, if you can call it a pause. Clouds passed over my head like in those stop motion films where an entire day is condensed into a couple seconds. I almost hung up the phone, figuring that by time I heard from Slowicki Sissy would already be dead of old age.

Eventually he picked up and told me what I didn't want to hear. All six slugs recovered came from the same gun – the one registered to Ariélle. "Okay," I said. "Thanks." He said something back, but it was hard to make out through the phlegm.

Damn! I closed my phone and while jamming it back in my coat glanced at my wristwatch. Double Damn! I was going to be late!

Call it a blessing, or pay-back from the Almighty, but an hour later I found myself at my destination in Toms River, a burb just across the bridge from Seaside. I parked at the curb in front of a run-down storefront and stared up at the faded metal sign hanging from a rusted pole over the front door: "Quality Bakery." I wish. The current name of the establishment, stenciled in lavender across the plate glass window was: "Miss Dorothy's Dance Studio."

Don't ask. Let's just say this had something to do with the night I proposed to Tina and woke up with un-wedded bliss smeared over my face. Didn't I already tell you men will do anything to get laid? But to be honest, it was more than that. I promised Tina we'd go out more, and I owed it to the kid. Of course I was only thinking of a nice dinner out. Tina was thinking of dance lessons. So we compromised and here I was at Miss Dorothy's lavender emblazoned dance studio.

With my chin on my chest I walked from my car like a condemned man to the gallows. Stepping inside I found myself on an expanse of green and gray floor tiles laid out in a checkerboard pattern. The wall at one end was one big mirror. Near it a gaggle of giggling five year old girls in tutus were huddling around their instructor, a pale pre-teen girl in a black leotard. The five year olds eyed me warily like nervous swans, and their puzzled instructor stepped forward and asked in an incredulous tone if I was here for dance lessons? Immediately a horrific image flashed through my brain. I saw myself in tights and a pink chiffon tutu balancing on one toe. "Oh God," I moaned to myself.

"Zolly?" I heard a voice call.

"Yes, dear God, take me now and spare me this final humiliation," I whispered toward heaven.

"Zolly, you're late. Miss Dorothy is waiting for us." I knew that voice. It wasn't God. It was the voice of someone far more demanding than the Creator of Heaven and Earth. I turned and saw Tina peeking through a curtain stretched over a doorway. "C'mon," she said urgently.

After glancing around the room for a noose and finding none, I walked through the curtain into a back room where Miss Dorothy was waiting for us. Miss Dorothy, or "Dot," as her friends called her, was born sometime during the last Ice Age. I was pretty sure that the only new dance she'd be able to teach us was the Minuet.

Dot claimed to have been a chorus girl on Broadway back in the day. I'd lay odds the day had a date with "B.C." after it. After retiring from the stage she moved to South Jersey and opened a dance studio in a former bakery. Here she made a

decent living scamming parents into believing their plump
daughters with bowling balls for feet were future ballerinas.

A sudden hacking cigarette cough focused my attention
on my inquisitor. She stood before me in a shiny saran wig
just one shade off cotton candy. Her foot tapped the floor
impatiently as ashes dripped from the butt dangling ever so
precariously from her lower lip. "Are we ready?" she asked,
totally devoid of enthusiasm. I thought for sure the cigarette
was doomed, but it clung miraculously to her lower lip as if
fastened there with crazy-glue.

"We're ready, Dot," Tina said excitedly. I looked over at
my baby's bubbly face and it made me smile. How could you
say "no" to this woman?

I'll spare you the ugly details of the next twenty minutes.
Let's just say Dante didn't know the meaning of the word
"Hell."

But then something amazing happened. Once I resigned
myself to my fate, I kinda relaxed. In a while I even got
accustomed to the smell of Jack Daniels on Dot's breath,
and to my surprise discovered the old broad still had it.
The spider's web of varicose veins on her legs made them
spring-like, and she bounced around the dance floor barking
instructions. Before I knew it I had Tina in my arms and the
two of us were gliding around a linoleum Shang-ra-la. I was
starting to have fun and even began to entertain the thought
of purchasing a top hat and tails.

CHAPTER TWELVE

You'd think that after making the supreme sacrifice and opening myself up to the humiliation of dance lessons Tina would have owed me big and I would have been richly rewarded that evening. Think again. Right after Dot's Tina rushed off to one of her many babysitting jobs. I could have tagged along, but couldn't face watching *The Little Mermaid* another five times. Although in the "feisty" mood I was in even the Little Mermaid was starting to look very very good to me. I found myself wondering what it would be like to do it with a chick who was half woman, half fish. It might not be at all bad, sort of a combination of sex and sushi.

Just as I was wondering how I was going to explain these impure thoughts to Father Gajendra, I got lucky in a different way. My cell phone rang. Oh God, I thought, please don't let it be Helen searching for human resources again. But it was good news. Really good news. The call was from Dandy Duggan the gym owner. He couldn't get the image of the woman he saw arguing with Kyle in the parking lot out of his head. He knew he'd seen her someplace before. It was another stroke of good luck that Dandy wasn't the greatest housekeeper. While sorting through a stack of newspapers that had accumulated over the past couple weeks something caught his eye. There on a front page was our Mystery Woman!

The next morning I was at the gym before it opened and found Dandy in his office whipping up his usual power breakfast in a blender. It was some gray concoction made with bananas, blue berries, wheat germ, and horse hair. Okay, I'm only guessing the hair was from a horse. Dandy insisted I try his witch's brew and rather than wasting time resisting I took one for the team. Wahhhhh! He forgot to tell me about the fish oil. It tasted as if I were drinking puree of Mackerel. If this was healthy living put me down for dying young.

But I suppose it was worth it. After I put my eyeballs back in their sockets Dandy took out a newspaper and showed me a photo of Ariélle and her entourage at the courthouse. "This is the dame I saw arguing with Kyle in the parking lot," he said definitively. I looked down. His finger was pointing to the face of Tammara King, Ariélle's pit bull manager.

After a pastrami omelet to counter the toxins from the health shake, I paid Guadalupe a visit at the Babylon. I found her cart beside an open door on the fifth floor and stepped in but didn't see anyone. Then I heard a stranger's voice behind me and grabbed a business card as I pivoted, preparing to concoct some excuse for being in the room. But once again no one was there and I soon realized the voice was coming from the TV. It was tuned to a Mexican game show named

"Surpriso Gigante" or something like that. Two sexy young women in scanty bikinis were pouring a bowl of chocolate syrup over a contestant's head. I couldn't tell if this meant he had lost or won. Suddenly there was a small gasp behind me and I turned to see Guadalupe emerging from the bathroom, grasping her heart.

"Santa Lucia! Mr. Zolly jou scare me!" After a moment to catch her breath Guadalupe found the TV remote and lowered the volume. "For a second I think you are my boss. He doesn't like it when I have the TV on, but I work just as hard jou can be sure of that."

I told her I was sure of that and made amends for giving her a fright by gifting her with a box of Johnson's Famous Caramel Corn from the boardwalk. Turns out she was a fan and happily munched away as we spoke. My kind of woman.

"What do you think?" I asked, pointing to Tammara King in the newspaper photo of Ariélle's entourage.

"Jes, that could be her."

"Are you sure? This is the woman you saw coming out of the murder room?"

"Hold your houses, I say 'could' be. It's confusing because when I see her she was wearing that 'none' scarf and sunglasses like this Ariélle woman is in this picture. Are they all members of the same order or something?"

I asked Guadalupe if it could have been Ariélle she saw leaving the murder scene, and she said the mystery woman looked more like Tammara King. But she couldn't be sure.

"I understand, I didn't mean to press you."

"This is really bothering me," Guadalupe said.

"Yeah, me too. I just can't seem to make the pieces fit."

"No, I mean I got some corn stuck between my teeth. Don't jou just hate when that happens? Jou got some floose or something?" she asked, picking at her teeth.

"Sorry, I'm out of floose."

"And I'm sorry I can't help jou. All I know is I think I see this muchacha coming out of 652." She pointed to Tammara again.

"And you don't remember what time that was?"

"You know, why didn't I think of this before?" she said, slapping her forehead. "Let me check my diary."

"You keep a diary?" I asked hopefully.

"No, I don't have a diary. Do you think I have time to write down things like 'what a beautiful sunrise, I found a leaf today, why is the sky blue?' I'm busy!"

"I understand."

"'Dear Diary, today was amazing, I cleaned twenty-seven toilets.'"

"Okay, I get it, I get it, you're a busy lady."

"I'm just yanking jour chin Mr. Zolly. I wish I could remember but I don't."

"That's okay, I know."

"And thank jou for the popcorn and all the food even if it makes me fat and no man will marry me and I get deported. Jou ever think of that?"

"It's on my mind constantly."

I called Tammara King and was lucky enough to find her in Ariélle's suite, even luckier she could spare a few minutes to talk to me. She was a busy lady too, exhausted from booking facials and dress fittings and planning which ski resort the family would spend Christmas at.

On the elevator ride up I kept thinking how this was a whole new ballgame. Was the mystery woman Guadalupe saw leaving Room 652 Tammara King? The very same woman Dandy had identified as fighting with Kyle in the parking lot? Was it possible she was having an affair with Kyle? Did Sissy find out or did Kyle confess and end the engagement? Either way it gave Sissy plenty of motive to pump good ole Kyle full of bullets. If only Guadalupe could remember if she saw the mystery woman before or after the murder.

I found Tammara in one of the rooms of Ariélle's suite that doubled as an office and her bedroom. She sat at a small desk stacked so high with ledgers, magazines and piles of papers that it looked like she was in a bunker.

"I'm sorry Zolly, but Ariélle always sleeps in after a show. You should have made an appointment or given me some warning you were coming," Tammara said, taking a moment to glance up from some kind of contract she was making notes on.

"Nah, that's okay. I don't need to see Ariélle. You're the person I want to talk to. It's kind of a sensitive matter."

"Oh?" she asked in an amused voice, surprised to hear how she could possibly be involved in anything sensitive. "Have a seat." She pointed to a hotel knock-off of a French antique chair, and I sat across from her, feeling a little bit like a kid talking to the principal.

"Understand that I make no judgments in these matters, that I'm just going with the facts as I learn them," I began.

"And those facts are?" She peered over the rims of her glasses at me.

"I've learned that Kyle Broder was cheating on Sissy. That he was seeing another woman."

"Really?" I could hear the skepticism in her voice.

"And... I believe that other woman is you." Bam! I let her have it right between the eyes and waited to see her reaction. Tammara stared at me for several long beats with a look more quizzical than startled. If the accusation had upset her in the least, it didn't show on her face. It wasn't a cliché, the woman *was* all business.

"And what's led you to that conclusion?"

"I have eye witnesses who say you two were a couple." Okay, it was only one witness and they hadn't actually used the word 'couple,' but to bring things to a boil you've gotta turn up the heat.

"That's very interesting. Who would say something like that?"

"That's not important right now." I didn't want to give her too many details. It was better to keep her guessing how much I had on her. To my surprise she turned back to the paperwork on her desk as if swatting away an inconsequential housefly.

"I admire your investigative skills, and your imagination, Mr. Michelangelo. But I'm afraid neither is going to be very helpful in this instance. The truth is I had been meeting with Kyle. The two of us were hammering out the terms of Sissy's prenuptial agreement."

"Don't the lawyers usually handle that stuff?"

"I've had some legal training, and we thought it would be more personal if I walked Kyle through the process."

More personal, yeah, like knowing the name and astrological sign of the shark circling you. "I see, well, that must have been difficult for you, having to come down hard on someone who's going to be family." As difficult, I thought, as an acetylene torch cutting through butter.

"Kyle was a reasonable guy."

"Really? Huh. 'Cause my witness says they saw you two in a pretty heated argument."

"Look, Mr. Michelangelo, Sissy will be inheriting a substantial sum of money someday and needs to be protected. Occasionally Kyle could be stubborn, but we all were working toward the same goal."

"Yeah, well maybe I jumped to conclusions." I wasn't believing this anymore than I believed my dentist when he said "You're only going to feel a slight pinch." But I didn't have enough to back me up and press further. And since she wasn't falling for my bluff there was no point seeking a confrontation.

"I guess you did," she said.

"Nothing personal, you understand I gotta follow every lead."

"Of course." She spoke without looking up at me. "Is there anything else I can do for you? Are you sure you don't need to speak to Ariélle?"

Speak to Ariélle? Was this her way of finding out if I was gonna blab my suspicions to her boss? Did that make her just a little nervous? Maybe I had gotten to her a tiny bit. If I was right she'd spent the entire conversation staring at the same paragraph on the contract before her.

"Nah, no need to trouble Ariélle," I said with a smile. "At this point," I added, giving her a little barb. Ha! I was really enjoying making the pit bull squirm. Maybe it was payback for that Chihuahua that bit my ankle when I was seven.

The phone rang on Tammara's desk and I saw her flinch a little. Ha! I really had her going now. Her hand was a little shaky as it reached out to pick up the receiver. "Tammara King." Her eyes darted to a corner of the room to avoid my own. "Yes, well, I'm afraid this is a bad time... I'm with someone... Didn't I tell you I... we can talk about it later... yes I'll be there at five...Yes, fine. Goodbye."

She hung up the phone looking as if the I.R.S. had called to schedule an audit. Lost in thought her eyes drifted back and registered surprise that I was still sitting there. "Will there be anything else Mr. Michelangelo?" she asked dryly.

Oh yeah, there would be plenty else, but I wasn't going to tell her that now. "No. Thanks for your time. I'll find my way out." She nodded officiously and I exited into the suite's living room. There I found Marshall in the kitchen pouring himself some orange juice. I couldn't tell whether he was on his way in for the morning, or on his way out from the previous night. But one thing I could be sure of, Marshall would be with Ariélle at show time if not sooner. So I decided to do an end run around the pit bull.

"Good morning, Marshall."

"Well if it isn't the I-talian with the great hair. Morning to ya."

"Listen, Marshall, I'm guessing you're very loyal to Ariélle."

"As loyal as a blind baby pig to its momma's teat."

"Excellent. I share that loyalty and I'm trying to do what's best for Ariélle. So I'm going to ask you for a favor."

"Mmm, I like being owed a favor." He started to grin like a cat that's cornered a mouse. I know, I know, I'm not homophobic, and we're supposed to be adult about this stuff, but I started to feel flush. He put down his glass and gave me his rapt attention.

"Yeah, good." I wrote something on my note pad, tore it out, folded it a couple times and handed it to him. "I need you to give this note to Ariélle when you see her, and don't tell *anyone* about it. Not Tammara, nobody."

"Oh, this is like an old black and white spy movie. I love the intrigue. But if I'm going to do you a favor it'll have to be tit for tat." I definitely didn't want to hear the word "tit" in this situation. Marshall's smile grew bigger and he moved in so close I thought he was going to kiss me.

"Uh, what would that be?" I stammered.

"God I love pulling your string!" He gave out a big laugh and retreated a few feet.

"I know that, pulling my string, of course." I forced a laugh.

"All I want in return is a promise ya'll come into my salon and let me try a few things with your hair," Marshall continued, serious now. I looked at him a beat, the wheels in my head turning.

"Fine. The deal is you owe me one haircut."

"Deal!" He shook my hand so hard I'd have trouble holding a pen the rest of the day. I was about to leave for the emergency room when I thought of something else.

"Say Marshall, do you know by any chance what kind of car Tammara drives?"

"When she's here in town she usually has a rental."

I asked if he knew what she was renting now. He wiped some juice from his lips and thought about it. "The woman's not exactly what I'd call trendy. You can bet whatever she's driving it's boxy and most likely brown." He laughed at his own observation then gave me that look again. "What kind of car do you drive, Mr. Z?"

"A Mini-Cooper."

"Ah, very sexy. You're a man ripe with possibilities." Here again "sexy" and "ripe" were not words I wanted to hear in a conversation with another guy.

"Thanks," I said in my most un-sexy voice.

I left the Babylon drawing three conclusions. One: I should stop dressing so dapper because it was sending off the wrong signals. Two: Tammara King was lying through her crowns about her relationship with Kyle. And three: the unexpected phone call she took was definitely from someone and about something she didn't want me to learn about. She told the mystery caller she'd meet them at five o'clock. I decided I just might want to make that appointment with her.

To do that I had to identify her car so I could follow her. That was a job for Wonder Woman – or "Tina," as she is known in the non-superhero world. Putting on her secretary voice Tina called around the car rental agencies in town saying she was Tammara King and needed to discuss the rental agreement for Ariélle. Wonder Woman is truly a wonder and in short time found the Hertz lot handling the account. They had three cars currently rented to Ariélle. One was a Lincoln Town Car, one a Mustang convertible, and the third a Ford Aspire. Ah yeah, the Ford Aspire, the vehicle that aspires to be a real car. Ha! I made a guess that based on

personality and the pecking order good ole Tammara would
be driving the little engine that couldn't.

Tina explained to the Hertz people that there had been a
minor fender bender involving the Aspire and that the police
had discovered a discrepancy in the VIN number on the car
and the one listed on the rental agreement. In no time she
had the make, model, color, and license plate number.

All I had to do was park a couple rows over in the parking
structure and enjoy my Whopper and onion rings while I
waited. What a shame. This was the day I'd promised myself I
was gonna start eating healthy. But I was on the run and didn't
have time to pop home and steam some broccoli. As much as
I love it. Right. Broccoli tastes to me like that green stuff you
scrape off the insides of your refrigerator – only with less flavor.

Before I even had a chance to taste my strawberry shake
Tammara showed up and drove off in her tan Aspire. I
followed at a safe distance and was surprised to see her get on
the Parkway and head out of town. This chase was gonna be
longer than I thought. Luckily I had king-sized my Whopper
meal.

Whatever business Tammara had, she was keeping it at a safe
distance from Atlantic City. It was a full hour before we exited
the Parkway and drove into Avalon, a sleepy upscale beach town
where you could get a house right on the sugary white beach.
I'd always dreamed of owning a place here, and if I took all the
money I was going to make on this case and added it to the
treasury of the State of New Jersey I might be able to rent one

for a week. I followed Tammara down a narrow sand swept road in front of a line of houses sitting right on the water. She pulled into the driveway of a modern structure clad in weather-beaten wood shingles to make it look older and "sea-sidey."

I slumped in my seat to remain out of view and drove on to the end of the block before parking. From this vantage point I could check out the scene in the Red Demon's side-view mirror. I watched Tammara get out of her rental and stride briskly up a path of stone pavers to the front door. The woman always walked as if rushing into a corporate board room with some important news. Or as Guadalupe would put it, like she had a "steak up her ass." Tammara let herself in with a key. I couldn't tell if anyone was in the house already. There was no one sitting on the front porch, but there was a garage and somebody might already be parked inside.

As I kept my eye on the mirror I lowered the car windows to take in the great ocean air. Ah, there was nothing like it. I munched on the last couple onion rings then carefully wiped my hands into the white Burger King bag on the floor. I had just gotten my beauty detailed and didn't want a single crumb to ruin her perfection. Her shiny buffed hood gleamed like polished rubies before me. And after a dousing of industrial strength freshener she was odor free.

After thirty minutes of seeing no one coming or going I got out of the car and made my way stealthily down the street for a closer look. In my hand I carried one of my most important investigative tools - a clip board. A clip board makes you look official. Nobody questions what you're doing snooping around when you're carrying a clip board - especially if you're wearing a blue blazer and a stylish hat. And no one ever looks close enough to see it's holding nothing but some old bus schedules and blank census forms. On the front porch I pretended to push the doorbell, then peered in a front window as if innocently looking to see if anybody was home. All I could spot was a small living room decorated spartanly with some rattan furniture. I had to be more careful around the back because of the large sliding glass doors, but I edged my nose around the corner and got a glimpse of a kitchen and small dining area. On the table was a bottle of wine and two glasses, one still half full. A hall led to what must have been a bedroom or two but I couldn't see anything but closed doors. And the windows on that part of the house were the high skylight types to give the residents privacy. Besides that there was nothing. No clothes lying around, no framed family photos or mementos, nothing to personalize the place. The house gave me the distinct impression of a rented love nest – a secluded hide-a-way far from the prying eyes of Atlantic City.

Damn. There must be more to this Tammara chick than meets the eye. Maybe she was also a pit bull in bed. Because if my theory was right and Tammara was screwing Kyle, it sure didn't take her long to find a replacement lover. Assuming she didn't already have another lover while she was bopping Kyle. Maybe she had two, or three, or more. My mind started to picture a three ring circus with a troop of acrobats forming a human pyramid and – well, some things are really none of your business.

I headed back to my Mini Cooper whistling a calliope tune and as I got closer noticed something odd. There was some kind of movement *inside* the car. I quickened my pace and soon could make out the movement as something white, something flapping… flapping like wings! I ran to my baby, gripped the door handle and peered inside in horror. "Nooooooooo!!!!!!!" My agonized scream echoed off the mountain tops. Well it would have, had I not been at sea level.

Inside a seagull with a thirty foot wingspan was flapping and hopping all over the upholstery as it tore open the Burger King bag to get at the scraps inside. "Noooooooo!!!" I shouted at the albatross, leaning in the car window and trying to shoo it away. The bird gave me an ominous Hitchcockian stare and continued to chew on the Whopper bun bouncing in its beak as it squawked at me defensively. Half in, half out of the car my rump waved in the air as I took off my hat and swatted at the albatross. It leapt up and fluttered around the front seat as my fedora struck empty air. As the bird perched on the steering wheel with a gleeful, taunting glare I swung once again, missed, and watched in horror as my fist pounded the horn. It sounded a loud "Whaaarrrrrrrrrr!!!" that startled the gull and it dove for my face. Able to duck at the last second, the feathered fiend flew over my head out the window and soared high into the air still clutching its precious flame broiled carrion. As I pulled my torso out of the car and stood upright I caught something out of the corner of my eye. A figure was coming out of the house. Tammara. Shit! Frozen in the doorway, her head was turned in the direction of the horn honk. Quickly I dove around the front of the car and crouched behind the bumper. Had she seen me? I was a block away and standing in the glare of the sun behind me. Even if she had she seen me, could she have identified me at this distance? I knew she didn't know what kind of car I drove. After another few seconds I peered around the fender of the Red Demon and was relieved to see Tammara get in her Aspire and drive off. Marone!

I waited till she was out of sight, then grabbing my chest walked around to peer inside the car and assess the damages. To my surprise there were no claw marks gouged in the upholstery, or any droppings splattered around the cabin. Not even a feather. With a sigh of relief I popped a couple Maalox, got in behind the wheel and collapsed against the seat in exhaustion.

As I casually stared out the sparkling clean windshield a small black speck appeared on the horizon. The speck grew larger as it approached with ferocious velocity and turned from black to white! Like a heat seeking missile it closed on me, aiming like a laser for a spot right between my eyes! Faster and faster. Closer and closer! I covered my face with my arms and BOOM! At the last second, inches from the windshield it veered sharply up and shot over the roof. The car shook. With sweaty palms and white knuckles I clutched the steering wheel. I craned my neck to look out the rear window just in time to see the feathered rocket disappear into the heavens. I closed my eyes and sighed in relief once again, having literally dodged a bullet.

And then I heard it. Thump. My eyes flashed open and focused in disbelief at the car hood where the remains of a Whopper teetered after impact. I scanned the skies to locate the bomber and – Plunk! Slunk! Sploptttttt! Splat!!! We took another hit. In horror I watched a heavy mass of gull crap explode on the hood like an erupting volcano. As it spread in an ever widening circle I could literally see the acidy glob dissolve the gleaming wax finish and eat away the ruby red paint. What the hell was up with my Mini Cooper and animal excrement?! I felt like some kind of reverse Noah – a man singled out and reviled by the animal kingdom.

My first instinct was to call 911 and summon the paramedics to treat the Red Demon's wounds. Or barring that, hurry to the closest car wash. But I couldn't leave. I needed to see who would come out of the love nest next. Tammara's lover might have nothing to do with anything, but you never know when the smallest detail could turn a case.

When I was sure Tammara was long gone I jumped out and tried to dress the burn the best I could with a bottle of spray cleaner and small chamois I keep in the first aid kit in the trunk. Then I sat behind the wheel and waited. Fifteen minutes. Twenty. I had to turn the radio on to drown out the sound of the acid bubbling away the paint. Or at least what I imagined to be the sound. Thirty minutes. Forty. I stared at the hood and was certain I could see the engine block under the disappearing metal.

In my mind I contemplated the long bridge that connected the mainland to the island where Seaside Heights and my apartment were located. I began to calculate the tensile strength of the metal guard rails and at what speed I would need to be going to ram through and plunge into the bay far below. It was then that my Creator intervened. Something caught my eye in the rear view mirror. The tan Aspire. Tammara was back. And she wasn't alone.

She parked her car at the curb this time, and a blue, windowless utility van pulled into the driveway close to the garage door. Two men got out and followed Tammara into the house. One was beefy and wore Dockers and a baseball cap. The smaller, frail looking guy had on jeans and a gray hoodie that covered his head and most of his face. It must have been eighty degrees out, but I guess style was more important to him than sweating.

Holy crap. This Tammara chick had one guy in the house already and now was bringing two more. What's the French term for that? A ménage a four? These people were definitely registering way off my kink charts.

On the other hand they could just be plumbers or electricians. Even though they weren't wearing uniforms, and instead of tools they were carrying a couple six packs. I spent the next thirty minutes contemplating the wiring and re-piping going on in the bedroom. Okay, I'm a man. I've already admitted that. But my instincts were right. In a few minutes the foursome emerged from the house. The beefy guy in the cap and the thin frail guy in the hoodie were joined by a blonde haired guy who looked like he couldn't be more than sixteen. Marone.

Hoodie and jail bait got in the van, but the beefy guy lingered and Tammara gave him a long hug and kiss before reluctantly parting. Then the Aspire and the van pulled away and went their separate ways.

Alone again, I got out to give the Red Demon's hood one final wipe, and heard cackling. I was sure it was the gods laughing at my vanity, but when I looked up I saw a gull sitting on a power line. I couldn't be sure it was the same gull that had attacked me, but why else was he laughing and giving me the evil eye? In a second he was joined by another gull, then five, ten, twenty! All giving me the evil eye like my grandmother Strega Nona used to give the meter reader.

As the chorus of cackles grew louder I jumped in the car, rifled through the glove compartment, and tossed a Milky Way bar out the window as a peace offering. As I rolled up the window and sped away I watched in the rear view mirror as the gulls swarmed over the candy, ripping the wrapper to shreds before tearing into the soft flesh below. At that moment I mentally crossed "parakeet" off my list of potential pets.

CHAPTER THIRTEEN

It was time to check out the dead guy's apartment. I always say you can learn a lot about a man by looking at where he sleeps. Who knows, I might even get lucky and find out *who* he was sleeping with.

I called Slowicki to get the address off the police report. I now owed him two subs and was beginning to feel guilty for contributing to his imminent heart attack.

Whatever Kyle Broder was blowing on cars and clothes, he sure wasn't spending any of it on his apartment. The place was one of those utilitarian, concrete bunker deals slapped together to squeeze out every penny it could for some rich podiatrist's investment portfolio. To be fair, I do have to add that it had a great view of a Shell Station and a noisy highway. Even given the drawbacks of Sissy's hotel room, this wasn't the kind of love nest she'd want to spend any time in. I'm betting she wouldn't even feel safe taking her clothes off in the shower.

I parked the Red Demon and grabbed my clip board. Kyle's apartment was on the first floor. As I stood in front of its peeling gray door I glanced around and saw nobody was

watching. Then son of a gun what do you know? The skeleton
key I was carrying just happened to fit his lock!

Inside the place was like a spread in *Architectural Digest*
– the Calcutta edition. What furnishings existed were the
pressboard crap you'd get at a discount furniture store. The
kind where the owner dresses up like a bunny or a pirate and
does his own ads on late night cable. The crap was accented
by some bad poster art of sunsets and horses. Within seconds
I was able to come to an important conclusion: Kyle – may
he rest in peace – was a slob. Newspapers, beer bottles, and
leftovers from McDonalds were strewn about as if a tornado
had hit the place. I found a mountain of old body builder
magazines on top of what you'd discover to be a coffee table
if you dug deep enough. Kyle's name was on the mailing
labels so it was a good bet the place hadn't already been re-
rented. Besides, it would have taken a new tenant a decade
to build the trash up to this level.

Venturing perilously further I found two bedrooms.
Because the smaller one looked relatively neat and clean I
figured it was reserved for guests and headed into the larger.
In this room the guy had splurged on the decor. The motif
was late twentieth century Ikea. On one wall was a queen
size futon and beside it a nightstand that leaned to the right
because whoever put it together wasn't too handy with an
allen wrench. Across from that a small Danish desk was
covered with an avalanche of opened mail, notes scrawled on
scraps of paper, and a pile of large manila envelopes labeled

"receipts." It was obvious Kyle was using the same system of organization I'd seen Orangutans at the zoo perfect with a roll of toilet paper.

Digging through the stuff I found a car wash coupon, an article torn out of a health magazine about protein drinks, and a curious piece of white cardstock like the laundry puts between shirts. On this "Kyle Broder" had been written about twenty times in varying degrees of size and neatness. Either the guy was taking a correspondence course in penmanship or he liked to see his name.

As I sifted through more junk the pile of manila envelopes began to teeter. I grabbed a fat one in mid-air and its overstuffed contents began to fall out like a mini ticker tape parade. At that exact moment my attention was drawn to a very unwelcome sound. The front door to the apartment was opening. Damn! I cocked my ear and heard something roll in, followed by the crash of a key ring being tossed into a dish. The normal human response to a predicament like this would have been to flee or hide, but being the quick thinker I am, I headed straight for the living room. "Hello?" I called out loudly.

"Who's there?!" came back a defensive male voice. I turned the corner and found myself confronted by a beefy young man built like a wrestler. The fierce look in his eyes told me he was poised to fight till the death; but despite having twenty years, fifty pounds, and a foot on me, I didn't flinch. I knew I could take him, especially since he made the strategic mistake of approaching me in a wheelchair. It also didn't hurt that his entire leg was in a cast from torso to ankle. It extended from his body at a ninety degree angle like a battering ram.

"Excuse me, I was told nobody was home," I said, putting on a professional smile and flourishing my clipboard.

"Who are you and what the hell are you doing in my apartment?" the wrestler asked, feeling more curious than threatened now.

"Lou D'Angelo, Exclusive Properties." I handed him a business card. "I'm appraising this property for potential acquisition by a client." Immediately I moved to the nearest wall and began tapping it with my knuckle. "Ummm, you hear that? Not good, not good at all."

"I didn't know the building was for sale."

"Landlords like to keep it a secret. They don't want tenants fleeing because they think the rent's going up."

"Is it?" He suddenly looked very concerned.

"I'm not in a position to know, sir. But when the heck did you ever hear of rent going down?" Without waiting for his reaction I smoothed my hand over the plaster. "Oh yeah, damp to the touch, a definite sign of mold. How long have you noticed it?"

"What? I never noticed anything."

"Well how long have you lived here?"

"About a year," he said, a little confused.

"Criminy, a year, and you never smelled nothing?"

"No. Is there something unhealthful I should be worried about?"

I frowned and thought a moment. "It really doesn't matter, you'll probably be moving out when they raise the rent. But to err on the side of caution I'd get my lungs x-rayed."

"So they *are* raising the rent?"

"You didn't hear it from me Mr. ...uh..." I glanced down at my clip board to consult some non-existent document. "Mr. Broder. Or can I call you Kyle?"

"Huh? Oh, no, I'm not Kyle."

"Really? Then there must be some mistake, the copy of the lease I got has this apartment rented to a Kyle Broder."

"Oh shit," he said with a heavy sigh. "Are they going to kick me out?"

"Why would they do that?"

"Well, because I'm not officially the one who rented the place. I'm Lucas... Lucas Broder. Kyle's my brother." A look of grief crossed his face. "Was my brother – I just lost him."

"My condolences."

"Yeah, thanks."

"I'm sorry to have troubled you at a time like this." My face assumed expression number seven – sincere sadness and sympathy.

"No problem." His eyes had that far-away look and I could see he was shaken by the death.

"Hey, you look like a good kid so I'm gonna give you a little legal advice. Always put all the renters' names on the lease."

"Yeah," he said softly. "But I never thought I'd be living here. It was Kyle's apartment. He let me move in with him after my accident. I didn't have insurance and if it weren't for Kyle footing the bills I would have been up shit's creak.... Jesus!" he said with a sudden realization. "Do you really think I'm going to have to move?"

I put my hand on his shoulder reassuringly. "I've seen a lot of these situations, and my advice is to get yourself a good lawyer. You being handicapped and all, no judge is likely to toss you out."

"Thanks," he said, a little relieved. "I appreciate the advice."

"You're welcome." I turned and started for the door, then turned back to him. "Say, maybe you could do me a little favor?"

"Sure, if I can."

"Do you know this woman?" I took out the newspaper photo of Tammara King Dandy had given me at the gym. I had put it inside plastic laminate to protect it, but more importantly to create "Zolly's Famous Fingerprints Trap" - patent pending. Anybody holding the picture would leave some nice fat prints on the plastic. The kid took the bait and grabbed the photo. I could tell immediately that he recognized the subject as he looked surprised, to say the least.

"That's, that's Tammara," he stuttered. "What....?"

"So you know her?"

"Yeah, well, kind of, whenever she came around I left Kyle and her alone."

"Oh, so she was his girlfriend?"

The kid answered with a big laugh then began to eye me warily. I felt like a haughty cat that got his paw stuck in a can and suddenly realized he wasn't as clever as he imagined.

"Who the hell are you?" the wrestler asked, sounding suspicious.

"Kid, it's better you don't know. The world of international real estate can be a very dangerous place for the uninitiated." I gave him a knowing nod and exited the door. Fortuitously I still had the manila envelope marked "receipts" tucked under my clip board.

Back in my car I was feeling pretty proud of myself. I was building a case that Kyle and Tammara were fooling around behind Sissy's back. Of course that meant I was also building a case that Sissy had a perfect motive to shoot the bum. "Ish ta nem!" That's Hungarian for "Marone!"

I popped a couple ant-acids and checked my voice mail. There was a message from Ariélle! Calling me directly! Marshall must have delivered the note telling her we needed to speak. I eagerly played back the message like a kid on Christmas morning. I was expecting a pony but instead got pony shit. Ariélle left a curt message to meet her in her dressing room before her show that evening. She sounded more than a little pissed. Huh... Well what was I expecting? It wasn't like we were friends or anything. This was a business relationship.

I had to cut across the backstage area to get to the dressing room. As I traversed a seemingly endless plain of hardwood, I paused to stare up into the rafters hanging high above me like the ceiling of a cathedral. It was then I realized how cavernous the stage was, and what an enormous, special talent it took for one brave human being to fill it with her talent. No, Ariélle wasn't like the rest of us. I was kidding myself. I didn't really know her at all.

As I reached out to knock on the dressing room door I felt a yank on my shoulder strong enough to spin me around, and found myself staring into the canines of a very angry pit bull. "I thought you understood the rules!" Tammara growled. "No one talks to Ariélle without going through me!"

"What are you afraid of?" I fired back.

"This is not how things are done. I won't tolerate it!"

"And I won't tolerate bullshit!" I shouted through clenched teeth. "I've been to Kyle's apartment. I've talked to his brother. He's the second person to tell me the two of you were fooling around behind Sissy's back."

Tammara let go of my shoulder. She looked stunned and I could smell blood. "Is that what happened?! Did Sissy find out and go nuts?!"

"That is ridiculous on so many levels!" She threw her arms down in frustration and retreated a step.

"Are you going to lie? To save your job you'll let Sissy take a premeditated murder rap?"

"I would never hurt Sissy." Her voice grew quiet. "What you're saying makes no sense. If I were having an affair with Kyle and Sissy found out, don't you think she'd tell her mother and I'd lose my job immediately?"

"*If* Sissy knew it was you. She might have learned Kyle was cheating, but not the particulars."

Tammara's voice rose, becoming deliberate and threatening again. "Don't mess with me Zolly!" And with that she disappeared into the darkness of the wings.

After walking off my anger I finally knocked on the dressing room door and was invited in by Marshall. He had just finished Ariélle's hair for the show and the two of them were laughing over the latest bad CD release from one of the "flavor of the week" girl singers. Ariélle asked Marshall if he could give us some time alone and he exited, winking and miming two fingers cutting through my hair like a pair of scissors.

Once alone I told Ariélle about the evidence I'd gathered pointing to an affair between her son-in-law to be and her manager. Ariélle sat and listened, as quiet and still as the pictogram of an Egyptian Queen on the wall of an ancient temple. When I finished she looked at me calmly, her lips barely parting as she spoke. "Zhat is not possible," was all she said. I asked her how she knew that and she answered simply "I know."

What the hell was it with all these cryptic answers? I was frustrated and some of the anger I'd felt just minutes ago began to return. I pressed Ariélle to tell me the truth, and when I was rebuffed I laid it out for her: "If you're not going to be completely honest and tell me everything you know, well then we're just wasting each other's time."

Ariélle was conciliatory and told me how much she appreciated my hard work. She would do everything she could to help me – short of involving the innocent. "That's too bad," I said reluctantly. And then the unthinkable happened. I felt my lips moving and from out of nowhere heard the words "I quit."

Had I actually said it? At that moment I suddenly knew how Lucifer must have felt falling from the company of angels.

"Is zere anything I can do to perzuade you to change your mind?" Ariélle asked calmly. I weighed my fall from grace with the alternative. Above everything else I was a professional. I did my job the way I believed was right, win or lose. My mind was made up, but I figured I'd test just how forthcoming Ariélle was willing to be.

"I've been a fan of yours all my life," I confessed. "But there has always been one thing that's driven me crazy."

"Yes?"

"That accent. Tell me where it's from, where you were born and I'll feel I can really trust you."

Her eyes widened and she gazed at me intensely. "Ariélle iz an ethereal flame fueled by mystery. Would you steal zhat mystery and eztinguish the flame? Is zhat what you wish, Zahlee, to eztinguish me?"

A thousand visions of what I yearned to do to her flashed through my brain. But being the kind of guy I am, dammit, I shook my head and said "No, of course not." Then to show there were no hard feelings about my sudden unemployment I graciously accepted an invitation to catch her show.

I made my way to the front of the showroom and an usher directed me to my seat front row center. It was one of those incredible "house" seats reserved by performers and the casino for V.I.P.'s. I tried to buy one of these from a scalper once and the price wasn't too unreasonable – just a few hundred bucks and my first born child.

I should have been in seventh heaven, but was feeling crappy about quitting. I also couldn't stop thinking about the case. Something Tammara said backstage stuck with me. If Sissy had caught her fooling around with Kyle, why wouldn't she have gotten her fired? And how could Sissy *not* have known it was Tammara? Wasn't she the mystery woman Guadalupe had seen leaving the murder scene? Didn't Sissy walk in on Tammara and Kyle? Unless...

Suddenly there was a crash of cymbals. No, it wasn't because I had a brilliant epiphany; it was an actual crash of cymbals from the orchestra. The showroom lights dimmed and a voice that seemed to echo from the heavens introduced

Ariélle. The audience began to applaud wildly and I decided that if this was to be the last time I saw my dream girl I might as well relax and enjoy myself.

The curtains parted on a pitch black stage. Then a single shaft of light bolted through the darkness, illuminating two eyes that glowed like amber flames. Those eyes. From that very first moment they seemed to lock onto my own and never once through the entire show lose contact. I grabbed the arm of my chair, spellbound.

The shaft of light widened to reveal a face of alabaster marble, its fine lips chiseled in an eternal pout. The face seemed almost mask-like – an ancient rendering of Nefertiti, Venus, Helen of Troy - the universal, timeless, quintessential female.

The light began to pulse and dart helter-skelter to discover a breast, knee, torso, arm, leg, and the heavenly voice reverberated again with a single name: "Ariélle! Ariélle! Ariélle!"

She wore nothing but a cat suit, the black Lycra conforming so tightly to every curve of her body it could best be described as "paint." She sat on a bare stage, legs folded under, her un-earthly long arms twisting up up up around her torso like vines reaching for the sun. The illusion of an exquisite flower.

The stage filled now with intense white light that poured over her body like the sun, warming and coaxing it to life. The arms untwisted and peeled slowly down as if the unfolding petals of an ebony orchid. Her legs straightened and she rose like a spring shoot onto her feet. With a musical blast Ariélle strode defiantly down the stage and burst into her trademark hit "I Am Alive."

For the next seventy minutes *I* was alive. I was fourteen again and sat mesmerized as Ariélle danced and sang like a woman half her age. Just when I thought things couldn't get any hotter I was proved literally wrong. Ariélle emerged in a gown of scarlet sequins, a slit running from below her ankle to the North Pole. The stage turned red and actual flames shot from pyrotechnic pots. Ariélle exploded into an old classic "Heat Wave," and with her hair and hips whipped three boy dancers into a frenzy of desire before reducing them to ashes.

When the peals of applause finally subsided, Ariélle, her chest still heaving, came to the edge of the stage. With a growl she walked down a small set of stairs into the audience and stood directly before – me! "Did you enjoy my little conflagration?" she asked in a deep voice made even raspier from her work out. The audience responded with wild applause and whistles. And then it happened. Ariélle looked down and stared right into my eyes. "Do you enjoy it when I sing?" she asked.

"Ye-es" I croaked like a thirteen year old whose voice is cracking.

"Do you enjoy it when I dance?"

"Ye-es," I said, the word squeezing out my throat.

"Do you like it when I do this?" She took a seat on my lap. I was touching Ariélle! I could feel the weight of her soft body across my legs.

"Oh God yes!" I answered, almost shouting. A huge laugh rolled over the crowd like a tidal wave.

"And tell me, do you like it when I do this?" She leaned in to give me a long kiss on my cheek. My face turned red and then redder, like the bulb of a thermometer about to burst. And suddenly I heard ringing!! Was it the blood pulsing in my eardrums? Was it my heart vibrating in my chest? Was it a chorus of heavenly angels calling me home?

No. It was my cell phone. Ringing inside my blazer pocket. The crowd erupted with an even bigger laugh. I froze. "Are you expecting an important call?" Ariélle asked.

"No," I gasped, the sweat cascading down my forehead like Victoria Falls. But the damn thing kept ringing. With a sly grin Ariélle's palm slipped into my blazer, extracted the phone and flipped it open.

"Hello" she said in a breathy voice that captured on a CD could have sold a million copies even without music. "Oh," she said, handing the phone to me. "It's Helen."

I grabbed the phone, spit out: "Not a good time," and slammed it shut. The audience was about to piss themselves.

"Who's Helen?" Ariélle asked coyly.

"Nobody," I grunted.

"Is Helen your girlfriend?"

"No!" I said instantly and decisively.

"Do you have a girlfriend?" she grinned. The lie took longer, but finally I shook my head and said:

"No." Okay it was a little white lie, like the Mendenhall Glacier is a little white snowball. But I'd asked Tina to be my wife over and over. Was it my fault she insisted on leaving me unattached and an object of desire for other women?

"Zen I will be your girlfriend tonight," Ariélle said rising off my lap. "This song is for...you." I sat transfixed, forgetting I was in a crowded show room, forgetting my own name, forgetting how even to breathe, as Ariélle sang a slow torrid ballad directly to me. Surprisingly enough, it was entitled: "You."

When I thirst,

you quench me.

Ariélle's fingertips danced across my lips.

When I burn,

you are ice.

Her palm pressed over my forehead as if checking for a fever. No need.

When I ache,

The orchestra reached a crescendo as she placed her hand over her abdomen.

you are release.

The word "release" hissed from her lips like a slow escape of steam. Her body tensed and struck a defiant pose.

I was born naked

Taking my hands in hers, she lifted me to my feet.

and you clothed me.

Her arms wrapped around me, drawing my body to her own.

I was born naive,
and you taught me.
I was born empty,
and you filled me.

As she held my head tightly against her bosom I felt faint and about to smother. I prayed for God to take me then – there could be no better way to die. I was beginning to black out - or it may have been that my eyes were crushed against her costume – when Ariélle released me, flung her body back as if performing a tango step, and peered into my eyes overcome with emotion. I was overcome with something else. I won't go into it here.

If they took away
zee heavens and zee earth,
I could still go on,
because of you...

She lifted my hand and planted a kiss on it.

you...

Her lips bussed my forehead with another kiss.

you!

Her lips found my own and pressed tightly over them for what seemed an eternity. It wasn't necessary. By the first "you" I was back on the case.

In her dressing room later I was able to win a concession that would make my job easier. Ariélle gave me her direct cell phone number so I could reach her anytime I wanted without having to go through the pit bull.

I floated out of the hotel and somehow me and the Red Demon made it back to Seaside. I have no recollection of driving. By the time I arrived home it was almost one A.M. and I was exhausted. "Near" sex can be more of a workout than the real thing. Before this night I'd never understood the appeal of lap dances. Why would a guy want to get himself worked up into a frenzy, only to be left frustrated? And why to boot would anyone *pay* for the privilege? It was like shelling out four bucks for a double cafe latte just to watch the girl behind the counter drink it! It all confirmed a profound conclusion I'd reached years earlier – people are nuts! But now suddenly I was nuts like the rest! And I didn't care. My euphoria was only tainted by the nagging thought of how much I had been missing!

I turned onto my street and it was so dark I could hardly find my driveway. The last time the city replaced the streetlight it was a candle. But that's understandable – city hall's way too busy thinking up new things to tax.

Through drooping eyelids I finally spotted the drive and cut the wheel to turn in. Instantly my eyes popped open in horror as the headlights illuminated a hulking form directly in my path. "Ahhhhhhhhh," I screamed, slamming the brakes.

"Ahhhhhhhhh" came a return scream outside the car. Before me a man in a tattered army jacket stood frozen in mid-shriek. Clutching an aluminum chaise over his head he looked like a crazed King Kong about to toss a bus. It was Blinks, the rummy. My car had come so close to hitting him the front bumper was creasing his pants. And believe me it was the first crease they'd seen in years.

Blinks' eyes were as big as pie plates and flashed like a signal lamp on a battleship sending Morse code. He stood rigid for another moment, then almost as if being literally knocked over by a feather, gently fell over backwards. I jumped out of my car and crouched over his body sprawled on the gravel.

"Hosanna! Take me home Lord!" Blinks cried out. I helped him sit up and looked him over. He seemed more shocked than anything, though it was hard to tell since Blinks' usual expression was shock and bewilderment. As he gathered what there were to his wits he stared at me in anger. "What the hell?! You think you're Dale Earnhardt or somebody, driving like a maniac?!"

"Dale Earnhardt's dead." I informed him.

"Because he drove like a maniac!" Blinks snapped.

"Look man, I'm sorry. It's real dark and I didn't expect anybody to be out this late. What the hell are you doing here anyway?" My eyes glanced around and saw the chaise lounge he'd been carrying. *My* chaise lounge. "Dammit! Were you stealing my chair?!"

"It's your own fault."

"My fault?"

"Everybody else brings their stuff in at night. You're negligent."

"It was all the way up on the second story. How the hell did you get up there?"

"Climbed the trellis," he said matter-of-factly.

"Damn, you're in good shape for an old rummy."

"So it's not enough to run me over, you also gotta insult me? For your information I haven't had a drink in sixteen months. Could be seventeen, I don't have a watch."

"Look, you're right. I'm sorry. Are you okay?"

"Hard to tell. I'm not sure what 'okay' is anymore." He got to his feet and dusted himself off. I put my hand on his back.

"How did it come to this, man? Living on the street, surviving on petty theft?"

"The usual story. My business partner framed me for larceny so my wife would divorce me and marry him."

The usual story? "Uh huh. Well look. You sure you're okay?"

"I'm sure of nothing! But I guess."

"Good. Listen pal, have you ever thought of finding yourself a real job?"

"I tried, but something weird always happens. Whenever they ask for my home address I blank out... Could be because I don't have one. Who knows?"

"Uh huh. Maybe I can help you out with that." I told Blinks a friend owed me a favor for helping find her run-a-way kid. She managed a small motel on Route Thirty-seven and would give him a place to put up till he got on his feet again. Maybe I could help him out with some new clothes; he might even consider taking a shower.

"You must be really scared I'm gonna sue your ass off," he said. I took it as "thanks."

"Oh, one more thing," I cautioned. "This motel is clean and all, but it caters to, let's say, a specific clientele. What I'm saying is, if a lot of sexy women in hot pants ask if you want to party, it's not because they find you irresistible."

CHAPTER FOURTEEN

In an entire lifetime there are two or three moments that define a person, moments when a man has to prove what he's made of. They often take place during wartime or some great disaster like a mine cave-in. My moment had arrived.

My trial by fire wouldn't take place storming a beach in Normandy, but at a hot trendy club Tina found named "Climax." "Hot." "Trendy." The two things I loathed the most in this world. But I had to prove my love to Tina by taking her dancing in public. Or maybe I was just trying to relieve the guilt I felt over my "near sex" with Ariélle.

Now I know I said the dance lessons were okay and that I was even beginning to enjoy myself, but making a fool of myself in front of Dot was one thing. Doing it in front of Atlantic City's beautiful people was another. As I parked behind the Chatterbox to pick up Tina I seriously considered speeding off and joining the witness protection program. Sure I'd miss the sex, but how bad could a life of celibacy be? Priests do it. Well a good number of them.

But it was too late. Tina was coming out the back door and spotted me. Not wanting to miss fifteen seconds of work she'd brought her "stepping out" clothes to the job and changed into them after her shift. I took one look at her in that short black skirt and gold sequined top and any thoughts of celibacy flew out the window.

"Hey, Baby," she said, jumping in the car and leaning across to give me a big kiss. "I am so excited Zolly. I can't tell you how..."

She was cut off by the ringing of my cell phone inside my blazer. I gave her an "I'm sorry" look and answered it.

"Hello? ... Oh crap, yeah hello Helen.... No, I'm sorry this is a bad time again." I hung up and found Tina eyeing me suspiciously.

"Who's Helen?" she asked like a rattler coiling.

"Nobody. It's business."

"'Cause I keep getting calls on the company line from a woman named 'Christmas.' You're not opening presents behind my back, are you Zolly?"

"Don't be ridiculous." I squeezed her knee. "Would I be taking you to Atlantic City's hottest club if I didn't love you babe?"

"Oh wow I can't believe we're actually going! This is going to be so much fun!"

Fun. Well not exactly.

I handed my keys to the valet and he gave me one of those long "what is your kind doing here?" stares. We were off to a good start. But I adjusted the feather on my hat to the 'we're number one' position, and when Tina took my arm I felt like a million bucks again. Inside was as dark as a telemarketer's heart. I mean, a bat could get lost in this place, if he could afford the cover charge. Come to think of it a bat might have felt more welcome.

We inched forward a little, hugging the wall, and bumped into a podium jammed in a narrow entranceway. A tiny brass lamp shining on a reservations list illuminated the ghoulish face of the maître d' or whatever the fancy name is for the guy who seats you in a place like this. With the silent stony face of the "undead" he ripped off a check from his pad and handed it to someone or something lurking in the dark beside him.

This entity immediately led us into the black hole, with Tina trying desperately to keep up and me clinging to her hand. We threaded through a maze of tables packed so tightly together a putty knife couldn't slide between them. I stepped on more than a few toes and was met with muttered obscenities. But what the hell, it was too dark for them to see who was doing the stepping. After a couple I started to enjoy the pain I was inflicting.

We made a turn and suddenly in the distance I could make out a small circle of light. I was hoping it was the light at the tunnel you see when dying, but no such luck. When I squinted I could make out a woman in a yellow spotlight clinging to a microphone stand and whispering a torch song. At that moment I suddenly slammed into Tina and realized she had sat down. I sat next to her, the two of us jammed behind a small cocktail table so close my gut was hanging over the top. We were also wedged between two bodies on either side of us that I assumed were alive because I could feel their breath.

"Can you believe how chic this place is Zolly?! Oh wow this is so great!" Tina whispered, trying to yank her evening bag up between our pressed knees. It got stuck then broke free with a force that caused it to smack me under the chin.

"Great," I replied, wondering if we grew up using two different dictionaries.

There could have been a dozen people in the place or a thousand. It was too dark to see anybody but the singer making love to the chrome mike stand. Once and awhile I could see eyes glowing in the shadows, and suddenly knew what it would feel like to be on the African savanna surrounded by hungry lions.

There seemed to be a buffer around the girl singer in the distance so I was guessing there was a dance floor. Did that mean there was a show first and then dancing? I couldn't decide if that was a good or a bad thing. Sure, it gave me a momentary reprieve before having to literally face the music, but on the other hand it might be better to just jump in and take my punishment, like diving into an ice cold swimming pool.

"Zolly, get up baby," Tina whispered with alarm.

"Wha?" I grunted in disbelief.

"I gotta go to the little girls' room," she said, somehow magically extricating herself and disappearing into the abyss.

I stood and groped desperately toward her silhouette but she was gone. My heart sank, certain I'd never find her again in this life. As I sat back down my hand missed my own table and my pinky ended up swimming in somebody's drink. Then things really got fun.

The singer finished her song and suddenly there was applause and the lights came up. How can I describe the lights coming on suddenly in a place so pitch black? It was like someone pressed my face against the lens of a lighthouse and said "okay, you can open your eyes now." I thought I could smell my own retinas frying.

Gradually I healed enough to see the singer taking a bow. Then she did something odd. Her hand grabbed the top of her head and pulled her hair off! I squinted in horror. Oh, it wasn't her real hair. It was a wig. Her real hair was still there, short and mannish as it was. That was a relief. Check that. "Mannish" as in man? The chick was a man! In a dress. And lipstick. I would have given anything for it to be Halloween, but it wasn't.

I looked around the room to see if anyone else was as shocked as I was. Apparently not. The guys in the first row nearest the dance floor were all applauding and hooting wildly. The guys in the second row were all.... The guys in the third row... Okay, you get the picture. They were all guys. Everyone was a guy. Either I had just been drafted or I was in a gay bar.

Okay, don't panic, you're an adult Zolly. "Climax!" Holy crap I'm in a gay bar named "Climax!" Jeez Marie where was

Tina?! This was her fault! Always looking for the hot and trendy. She had no idea Studio 54 closed decades ago, why should she know she was taking me to a gay bar?! Where was she? We had to get out before somebody saw me... Wait. Who was gonna see me? Who would I know here. Ha ha. I laughed a little gallows laugh. Stay calm man. Tina will be back. We'll leave. That's when a guy to my right elbowed me. "Really great voice, don't you think?" he asked.

"The best," I answered, suddenly an expert on drag queens. *Where* was Tina? Don't panic. She always disappears into the ladies room for what seems like an hour. Holy crap! Did they even *have* a ladies' room in this place? Okay, relax, don't get crazy, don't call attention to yourself.

"Zolly!" a voice boomed behind me and I jumped six inches off my seat. An iron claw gripped my shoulder and my spine quivered like when I was a kid and the barber put his buzzing electric razor to the back of my bare neck. "Zolly!" the voice thundered again, and my name echoed through the club. Echoed with a Texas drawl. I turned to see Marshall, Ariélle's hairdresser, sliding into the seat vacated by Tina.

"That's that's my girlfriend's seat," I stammered.

"Oh my, darlin.'" Marshall tilted his head and gave me a sympathetic look. "Ya'll don't have to use that old excuse; I won't tell anyone I saw you here."

"I'm here with my girlfriend Tina, a real girl girlfriend, she's in the can." He placed his hand over mine on the table and stared in my eyes.

"It's okay, it's o-kay. Trust me Zolly, ya'll feel so much better when you finally come out."

Tina! I screamed inside my head, but she was nowhere to be seen. Deafening music started to blare and couples, the predominantly male kind, got up and began to dance schizophrenically to a pounding beat. I don't think dear old Dot had ever seen dancing like this, unless she worked in an electro-shock clinic. "Look Marshall, I'm not making judgments here, all I'm saying is I'm not gay."

"If that's how ya want to play it," Marshall said, sadly clicking his tongue. Then his finger stroked the feather on my hat curiously. "Ya'll wear your feather on the left side, is that some kinda code?" he asked with a wink. "Like wearing an earring on the left means you're..."

"There she is!" I cut him off and pointed across the room at Tina emerging beside the bar. Marshall's eyes followed my finger to her. "See? Do you believe me now?"

"My my, I *am* impressed. I'd love to get the name of the surgeon who did her work! That's the best looking tranny I've ever laid eyes on. You're a lucky man Mr. Z, you sly dog."

"Tranny...what? She didn't have any work done. She's a woman. And my girlfriend."

"That is really getting old sir. But hey, if you'd feel more comfortable in private I'll get my boyfriend and we can go back to my place. Is your man into foursomes?"

"Tina!" I shouted out. But she didn't hear me over the din. And she wasn't coming. Unbelievably she'd stop to talk to a young man in very tight jeans and a fringed suede shirt. Tina is the kind who can make friends anywhere. I swear she'd find someone to gab with fleeing a tsunami.

"Relax, Mr. Z," Marshall said, falling back in his chair. "I'm just yankin' your chain!" He gave out an interminable laugh that rumbled like a cherry bomb in a kettle drum. "I know you're as straight as a line between a wolf and a T-bone steak! Oh Lord, you are funny. I just love makin' ya'll squirm!"

"Yeah, me too, love it," I grumbled.

"Oh come on, don't get all pissy, I was just funnin' ya. Can ya forgive me?"

"Yeah, yeah," I said grudgingly.

"Alrighty. And don't ya'll forget I still owe you that haircut." He ran his fingers through my hair. "Have you ever thought of auburn highlights?"

"Actually I did once, but I was high on bug spray. Stop doing that!"

"Now I'm not gonna leave here with ya'll still angry. In exchange for getting your panties in a knot I'm going to help you out with somethin'."

"No need."

"It has to do with your case." I turned and could see Marshall was serious now.

"What? Do you know something?"

"I shoulda done told you earlier, but I'm not the kinda person who likes to butt into other people's business."

"Oh yeah, like giving them auburn highlights."

"Do ya'll want to hear or not?"

"What have you got?"

"Well this Kyle guy, Sissy's fiancée? He wasn't exactly the person he claimed to be."

"Was he fooling around with other women? I knew it!"

"Not exactly other women."

"Huh?" I shrugged. Sometimes I'm as dense as month old pudding in the back of the fridge.

"Good ole "straight" boy Kyle hit on me a couple times, and I could point out half a dozen guys in this room who took him up on the offer."

"Kyle was gay?" I asked. Marshall looked at me and nodded nonchalantly. Suddenly I was on that merry-go-round spinning out of control again. I was dizzy, but afraid to sit down because I didn't know the gender of the horses. "Why was he engaged to Sissy? What was his game?" I asked when my head cleared.

"Don't know."

"You seem pretty close to Ariélle, did you ever tell her what you just told me?"

"I thought about it, but never did. One thing I've learned workin' for these people Zolly, is no matter how much they claim ya'll "part of the family," you're just an employee. And shame on me, but I enjoyed all the perks that comes from hangin' out with Ariélle and didn't wanna risk losin' 'em.

Besides, Sissy's old enough to know what she's doing. Do ya'll think I'm a bad person?"

"Nah," I said, patting *his* hand this time. "You're one of the good guys."

Tina finally arrived at our table and I made introductions. She gave a little yelp of pain as I tugged her hair to prove it wasn't a wig. I thought of grabbing her boob but decided that was a step too far. Plus having a boob nowadays is no true test of gender, you can buy them off the rack – to make a bad pun. Tina insisted Marshall keep her seat then sat on my lap and whispered in my ear: "Zolly, do you think this is a gay club?"

I grinned and said "I thought you knew, baby."

Soon Marshall's boyfriend, a thin Japanese med student named Leo joined us. And in a little while they coaxed me and Tina onto the dance floor to teach us a couple of the latest steps. It was a hell of a lot of fun and we ended up dancing and laughing into the wee hours. Like I always say, when you start down a road you never know what cool place it's gonna lead you.

CHAPTER FIFTEEN

I didn't sleep much that night with all the questions and merry-go-round horses galloping through my brain. The next morning was one of the rare times I woke up before the workaholic Tina, and gazing at my angelic ballerina I didn't have the heart to wake her up by making noise in the kitchen. So I stepped out to grab a coffee and a crueller from my Uncle Gabor's bakery and took them up onto the boardwalk. For me sitting on a bench watching the sky and ocean was the best entertainment in the world.

It was a little before dawn and the place was deserted. As much as I find people watching fascinating, I also savor this time of day for its solitude - the stage empty of its actors. No one was gonna call you on the phone, no neighbor was gonna drop by unexpected; there was no place you had to be, no stores or post offices or dentists to rush to at this hour. It gave a guy time to think.

I dunked my crueller in the coffee and watched the first streak of pink light crack across the horizon. It looked to me as if the earth was lifting its eyelid. If only I could open *my* eyes. I was missing something. Missing the one piece of the puzzle that made everything else fit.

So Kyle was gay? Just when you think you've got a handle on a case, BAM! Somebody tosses a hand grenade into your logic. Okay, if Kyle was gay what did that mean? Did Sissy find out? Was that her motive for murder? Nah. She didn't seem all that choked up about losing Kyle to the Grim Reaper. If she didn't love the guy why would ending the engagement make her mad enough to kill him? Maybe she just didn't like the idea of losing?

But wait. If Kyle was gay, what was he doing fooling around with Tammara? From my experience people are motivated by three things: sex, money, and using the money to get more sex. So if Kyle and Tammara's relationship wasn't about sex, was it about money? Maybe it all *was* "business" as Tammara claimed. Were she and Kyle involved in some sort of scheme to bilk Ariélle? The guy was into fancy clothes and expensive cars. Dandy made a point of saying how the kid was living way above his means. Somebody had to pay for that.

When I got back to my apartment I found a note Tina left where I was sure to see it – the refrigerator. "Zol, I owe you big, Love T."

Ah it feels good to make someone happy. It feels even better if they owe you big. Better still if the person doing the owing is a hot chick. My mind began to race with ideas on how to collect, trying to keep the props and costumes required to a minimum. But being the professional I am, I soon turned back to what I was thinking about on the boardwalk: Kyle and living above one's means.

I retrieved the manila envelope I magically came into possession of at Kyle's apartment and emptied a blizzard of receipts onto my kitchen table. I spent the next hour going through the pile like it was an archeological dig. There were the usual bills: electric, gas, credit cards, car lease; and receipts for purchases from Sunoco Gas, sporting goods stores - all kinds of business deductions that would show up on his 1040 at the end of the year. There were also receipts and check stubs from clients paying for training. They were all made out to "GoForIt! Inc." which I guessed was the name of Kyle's private fitness business.

Most of the payments were for fifty, a hundred bucks worth of gut busting a pop. But there were two receipts from a corporation named "Aphrodite, Inc." that were a whole lot more interesting. One was for five grand and the other for ten. This Aphrodite person must have gotten one hell of a workout.

Aphrodite... goddess of love, beauty, lust... hmmm *lust*. That was something I knew about lusting over Ariélle the way I was. Wait! Aphrodite. 'A'... 'A' like in 'Ariélle?!' Could it be? I would have bet Grandma Rozsa's chicken paprikash recipe that it could. I called Ariélle's direct number and was lucky to catch her taking a steam bath. Or maybe it was 'unlucky' because the image of a naked, sweaty Ariélle was just a tad distracting. No, "tad distracting" was a mosquito buzzing your ear. This was a jumbo jet landing between my eyes.

But being the professional I am I sucked it up and pushed on. Ariélle told me that as a joke she had indeed named one of her many corporations Aphrodite, Inc. Eureka! For once having my mind in the gutter paid off.

When I told Ariélle her company had made a couple large payments to GoForIt! she had no idea what they were for. Bookkeeping was a boring task she relegated to Tammara and the accountants. When I told her GoForIt! was Kyle Broder's company she suddenly seemed a little less bored. And this time when I asked Ariélle to leave Tammara out of our discussion she didn't give me an argument. I think her trust in the pit bull had begun to fade just a bit.

Wondering what my next move should be I stared absentmindedly at the manila envelope marked "receipts" and recalled how this envelope had been in the pile teetering on Kyle's desk. It was the one I grabbed at random when it began to fall. I checked through the receipts again and realized all had been for the months May and June. That meant it was a good bet the envelopes left behind had receipts for other months of the year. Did they also contain large checks to Kyle? I asked Ariélle to contact her accountant directly and get me a list of all payments Aphrodite, Inc. had made to GoForIt! and she agreed. Yes! I was on a roll! For a second I got so cocky and thought about asking Ariélle if she was wearing a towel, but I quickly came to my senses, said my goodbyes and hung up.

It looked like my hunch was right. Tammara and Kyle were involved in some kind of scheme to bilk Ariélle. I was thinking about this, and about Ariélle toweling off when I was rudely interrupted by my phone. It was Slowicki.

"Hello, is your mommy home little boy?"

"No but *your* mom's here. I won't disturb her 'cause she's still in my bed basking in the afterglow." Even Slowicki had to laugh at that one. Well choke. But I could tell it was the laughing kind of choke.

He was calling because I was late picking him up. He had a dentist appointment and I always served as designated driver because to get Slowicki to the dentist required a quantity of drugs normally reserved for bringing down rogue elephants.

The afternoon was a picnic – like a picnic in a horror film invaded by giant ants. First Slowicki complained about having to cram his bulk into the Mini Cooper. "Damn Japanese cars!" he cursed.

"It's British," I informed him.

"Same thing," he said, needing to get in the last word. "How the hell is a human being supposed to fit in one of these pieces of shit? Do they come with a can opener?" After a lot of straining he managed to plop his ass inside, but his shoulder caught on the roof frame.

"Damn Slowicki, am I going to have to come out there and shove you in? Because this is starting to look like a clown act at Ringling Brothers."

"Errrrghmmmmmmmphhhhhhhh" he muttered, finally popping his over-sized body through the door frame. "Ouch, shit!" he exclaimed as his head hit the plastic dome lamp. "Son-of-a.... If I had two of these pieces of crap I might be able to use 'em as roller skates!"

"Tough luck about the root canal," I said to change the subject and get his goat.

"Who said anything about a root canal?!" His eyes widened in shock as he gaped at me.

"Sounds like you need a root canal to me, but hey, what the hell do I know I'm not a dentist."

"Yeah, what the hell do you know... root canal my ass. I probably just need a good clean..." He stopped in mid-sentence, his nose turning up like a pig sniffing truffles. "What the hell is that smell?"

"What smell?" I asked innocently.

"Hell. It's like that guy in booking who wears the piss bag. What's his name?"

I had to tell him the guy's name and explain the car had a slight odor because of a cat.

"A cat?! Dammit Zolly spring for some *human* companionship next time," he said with a smirk. "I know a girl works the bus station. I can loan you a few bucks if you're short." After a second he realized the pun he'd made. "Short?!

If you're short?!" He then erupted with a spray of laughter that made me wish I had windshield wipers *inside* the car.

"Oh, by the way," Slowicki said when his explosion subsided. "Those prints you gave me, I got a report back." He was talking about the prints off the plastic laminate I'd put around Tammara's picture and baited Lucas Broder with at his brother's apartment. Well it turned out that Lucas wasn't Kyle's brother – unless they had different fathers and different last names – because the name the computer kicked back as matching the prints was "Lucas *Nash*." He had a couple arrests in Ocean County for "indecent exposure." That meant he was discovered sharing a bathroom stall with another man at a rest stop on the Parkway. A very popular destination for gay men. You had to feel bad for them. While most young lovers have Paris and Niagara Falls gay guys are reduced to romantic get-a-ways in toilets.

But this put a new wrinkle on things. If Lucas Nash wasn't Kyle's brother who was he? Was he simply a good friend Kyle was sharing his apartment with in his time of need? Or was their relationship more like sharing a stall on the Parkway? And if the later was true, why was he still trying to protect Kyle's heterosexual image even after death? Or maybe it was his own ass he was trying to protect.

Slowicki took a bite out of a Baby Ruth bar and tossed the wrapper into the floor well. "Dammit Slowicki who the hell eats a candy bar on the way to the dentist?"

"What?" he grunted. "When better to break a tooth or lose a filling then on your way to see the man who can fix 'em? I say get all the damage in now."

"On the subject of damage could you *not* trash my car?" I watched as a cascade of peanut dust fluttered onto the upholstery.

"Excuse *me*," Slowicki said with dramatic emphasis. "I didn't know I was in a sterile environment. Are you going to drive the G.D. car or use it as a condom? Excuse *me*, this G.D. piece of shit ain't big enough to be a condom. "

It only took me a couple hours to get revenge. When I picked Slowicki up later and his face was all swollen and puffy and he was moaning in pain and dripping blood - I was crunching peanut brittle. I offered him some and he swore something at me. Which is when I discovered that even with a mouth full of cotton it was impossible for Slowicki to be less intelligible.

Then I gave Slowicki the "look." He returned it and nodded toward the road beyond the windshield. This was the end of the laughs for the day. As was our custom we drove to the cemetery where his wife Claire was laid to rest. It was best for this kind of trip that Slowicki was already sedated.

It was also our custom for Slowicki to kneel at the gravesite and say a prayer while I stood at a distance mulling over the events that lead to Claire's death and my leaving the force. Nah, they're wrong. Time doesn't heal all wounds.

The next afternoon I got a call from Ariélle. Her accountant had done a quick audit and found a total of seven checks issued to GoForIt! All had been cashed with the endorsement: "Kyle Broder, President." The checks had been drawn pretty much on a monthly basis starting in January. The first five were in the amount of five-thousand, but jumped to ten thousand in June. Then the amount doubled to twenty-thousand for the last check issued in July. July? I asked Ariélle if she had a date that last check was cashed. She did and it turned out to be two days after Kyle was killed. Either this was proof of life after death or something funny was going on.

I thought I knew the person who could answer that.

A short time later I was knocking on the door of Kyle's old apartment and was greeted not so warmly by his alleged half-brother Lucas. "Who the hell *are* you?" he asked. "I'm calling the cops dude."

"Good. It'll save me from having to call them."

"I'm not buying any more of your b.s." He reached up from his wheelchair and started to close the door on me.

"Okay, but maybe you'd like to explain something for me." I blocked the door with my foot. "How does a dead man endorse a check?"

"What?!" There was a long silence and I knew I had him. I could see the wheels spinning in his head as he searched for some kind of answer. "What the hell asylum did you escape from?" he finally asked, but the cockiness was gone from his voice. Ha! The poor schlub was no match for the master mind of Zolly Michelangelo.

"You endorsed that last check didn't you? That's why I found the paper where you were practicing Kyle's signature." He backed his chair into the apartment without answering and I followed.

"So you're a cop?" he said with resignation.

"A private cop."

"Look I'm screwed here. I've got no job, I need more surgery, and Kyle is gone. I found that check in Kyle's room while looking for his will. So I cashed it. What's the big deal, he was owed the money."

"You're right. From my experience the cops don't look at forgery and larceny as a big deal."

"What are you going to do?" he asked, looking me in the face for the first time. The guy was clearly more the victim of a lot of bad luck than a felon. I was beginning to feel sorry for him. We've already established I can be a sucker.

"That depends on how co-operative you are." He nodded his head in resignation and I dropped the bomb:

"Were you Kyle's lover?" His eyes flashed and he made a loud nervous laugh that rocked his torso in the chair.

"Are you kidding me man?"

"No, man. I know all about your arrests for indecent exposure on the Parkway."

"Go screw yourself!" he shouted, pivoting his chair and wheeling away.

"I'm asking you again, were you and Kyle lovers?"

"I don't care what the hell you tell the cops. Get out."

"Were you?"

"God dammit! Why can't you leave me alone? Isn't this enough?" His knuckles were white from gripping the metal rims of the chair wheels. "Isn't this enough?"

"That's a real bad break man, but not as bad a break as Kyle caught. Whether he was your lover or you two were just close like brothers, how can you let it go? How can you let somebody get away with murder?"

His eyes were welling with tears as he lifted his head. "I loved him. I swear."

I told him I understood and felt sorry for him. And this wasn't a Zolly scam. I meant it. Then I asked him to help me for Kyle's sake. Did he have any clue who would want to kill Kyle?

"I think the cops pretty much got it right." He believed Sissy killed Kyle. "The chick even confessed - what more do you need?

"Why? Why would she want to kill him?"

"That bitch!" he shouted, spitting the words. I was beginning to get the idea he didn't like Sissy. So I asked again why Sissy would want to kill Kyle.

"Who knows what goes on in that skank's head? She was getting everything she wanted." I asked if he was referring to their engagement and he said yes. So I went on to ask what that was all about. Why was Sissy marrying a gay guy? Or didn't she know.

"Are you kidding me, of course she knew. But what did it matter? Kyle was just a prop. She needed a husband, she bought a husband; it was like picking a dress off a rack – only Sissy would rather die than buy anything off the rack."

Lucas went on to tell me he didn't know why Sissy needed a husband at this particular moment. He wasn't even sure she needed a reason, it could have been as simple as her being jealous of all the lavish celebrity weddings splashed over the news lately, or that toy poodles were passé and husbands were the "must haves" this season. The more he talked the more his bitterness revealed itself. Forgive my tactics once again, but I brought things to a boil by asking how he felt that Kyle was abandoning him to marry Sissy.

Suffice it to say he wasn't happy. He suggested a few things Sissy could do to herself that seemed anatomically impossible. But I couldn't rule anything out. Remember the strap-on I found in Sissy's drawer? I was learning things that would scar me for life.

Lucas went on to tell how it all began when Sissy hired Kyle as a trainer. When training turned into "dating" Kyle kept it from him. It was only when Lucas began to suspect Kyle was sneaking around with another man that Kyle stunned him with a confession: yes he was seeing someone, but it wasn't another man, it was a woman. Even more shocking was Kyle's announcement he was planning on marrying the woman. Lucas was devastated but Kyle explained it was nothing more than a "marriage of expediency" and that he was doing it for Lucas. Sissy's money was the only way they could pay the astronomical medical bills and afford the operations the doctors told Lucas he would need if he ever wanted to walk again. Kyle swore he'd forget all about the marriage if Lucas could think of any other way, but Lucas had none to offer.

After the initial shock Lucas was grateful and loved Kyle even more for his sacrifice. But it wasn't long before the thought of sharing Kyle with a woman stuck in his craw like a stone that became sharper and sharper as it twisted inside him. Soon their relationship deteriorated into one big shouting match. A chasm opened between the men that neither seemed able to cross, with Lucas insisting they find some other way and Kyle intent on making the "big score." Kyle's death, coming at a time when the two were estranged, made it doubly painful for Lucas.

As he finished his story Lucas stared past me at the wall. It was a vacant stare mirroring what I think he saw as a vacant future.

I believed the sincerity of everything Lucas told me, but had a gnawing feeling there was something he wasn't telling me. The fact that he loved Kyle deeply was something to be admired, but could also end up damning him. Jealousy was a powerful motive and without realizing it Lucas had just added his name to my list of murder suspects. But was this simply an example of a spurned lover thinking "If I can't have him nobody can?" Or did Lucas come to believe that the "big score" wasn't solely for his benefit? The expensive clothes and fancy sports car made it pretty obvious that good ole Kyle had become addicted to the lifestyle Sissy provided him. Did Lucas come to believe that Kyle was betraying him not only to pay medical bills but to drive a BMW? Jealousy and greed. It's such an old story you think we'd have learned by now.

I didn't reveal any of these thoughts to Lucas. Instead I offered him my condolences again and told him if he remembered anything that might be helpful to give me a call." I handed him a business card and he glanced at it.

"Ramos Brothers. The termite experts?"

"Wrong card," I said with a guilty smirk.

CHAPTER SIXTEEN

"Did you know Kyle was gay?" Sissy stared at me as if I'd just told her Versace had gone out of business.

"That's a sick joke!" she shouted, tossing her Mercedes Benz catalog onto the coffee table with annoyance. Did this chick think her prison cell was going to come with a garage? "Why would you say something horrible like that?" She put on the rich girl pout she had learned in the womb. I couldn't tell if she was upset because the news shocked her or because I'd discovered the truth.

"So you didn't have any suspicions he was gay?"

"Of course not! Why would I get engaged to a gay man?! That is so passé! Do you think I'm stupid or something?!"

Oh boy. To answer that question I'd have to cut down every last remaining tree on the planet to make enough paper. I resisted the temptation to scream "Stupid can only be applied to organisms more evolved than amoeba!" Instead I said: "It wasn't my intent to insult you."

A look of panic crossed the one-celled creature's face. "You didn't tell Mommy did you?!"

"Not yet."

"Because it's so ridiculous... After everything she's been through I forbid you to upset her anymore. Poor Mommy. She was so happy to hear I was settling down... Are you a parent, Zolly? Can you understand the joy of giving your daughter away in marriage?"

Honey if you were my daughter I'd lead you down the aisle on a jet ski. "I'm not a parent, but I understand," I said.

"All these horrible things. We have to protect Mommy from any more heartache."

The time to do that had long passed. Somebody should have insisted Ariélle spring for amniosynthesis.

"Oh by the way," I said, baiting a trap. "I talked to the Coroner's office and they're ready to release Kyle's body."

"Uh huh," she mumbled, perplexed as to the relevance of what I'd told her.

"In case, you know, you want to make arrangements." It still didn't register with her. "For a funeral."

"Oh," she said flatly.

"Unless Lucas is already taking care of it."

"Lucas?" she asked, adrift in the Stupid Sea.

"Kyle's brother."

"Oh, yeah, right."

"You've been in touch with him haven't you?"

"Uh huh."

This was interesting news to me. She hadn't given a thought to arranging a funeral for the man she was supposedly in love with? And she didn't seem to even know the name of his brother? It all lent a lot of weight to Lucas' claim that this was nothing more than a marriage of expediency.

"Oh c'mon, don't look so down Zolly," Sissy said, noticing the deepening frown on my mug. "It's not all bad news."

"No?" I knew I was walking into a mine field but was too beaten down to save myself.

"All this murder stuff has led to a flood of offers." She picked a script off the coffee table and held it up proudly. "They want me to star in this TV pilot. Well not as a regular but I'd be the guest star in the first episode."

"That's great," I said, smiling and hurrying to leave before I received more information than I needed. But I wasn't quick enough. Like Pompeians fleeing the lava flow from Mt. Vesuvius I was trapped in a river of molten idiocy gushing from Sissy's mouth.

"It's called 'Celebrity Gynecologist,' and each week they follow around a different doctor and his celebrity patient as..."

I didn't hear the rest, or maybe I did and have blocked it out. All I can remember is going home and tossing my TV out the window.

Talking to Sissy had a way of increasing my stomach acid. It was that and possibly the fried peppers from the sausage sandwich I had for dinner that had my guts in a twist now. As I sat on my bench on the boardwalk fighting back the angina I committed an unforgivable sin - I threw away a half-eaten zeppole. I know, zeppoles, sausage sandwiches... I promised Tina I'd start eating better, but Tina had a babysitting gig and I was on my own. And if a zeppole falls in a forest and your girlfriend isn't there to see you eat it does it count?

"Hey YOU!" I felt a sudden slap across my back and twisted around on the bench to find Blinks standing before me. Only something was off. He was Blinks but he wasn't Blinks. Was it because thanks to a shower he no longer announced his presence five minutes before arriving. No, it had to do with his look. Yeah, he was wearing the pants and shirt I picked up at the thrift store, but there was something else. I couldn't quite put my finger on it.

"Hey pal, good to see ya," Blinks said, his constantly flashing eyes full of genuine gratitude. "I like my new room. I'm really stepping up in the world. This afternoon I applied for a janitor gig at the Wal-Mart."

"That's great. You're doing real good buddy."

"And," he said puffing out his chest proudly and standing back on his heels. "What do you think?"

I looked him over from head to toe, then back to head again. That was it! His hair was different, and not just washed. Different. He got his hair cut.

"Looks good, don't it pal? At first there I thought it wasn't gonna work out. I walked into that fancy salon and people looked at me like they never seen a guy coming for a haircut. I'm telling you it was a weird place. There were all these ladies with strips of aluminum foil in their hair. Freaked me out. I had a friend named Beans in re-hab, and he used to wear an aluminum foil hat to keep the C.I.A. from using mind control on him. You think those ladies are doing the same, pal?"

"I wouldn't be surprised. What other logical explanation could there be?"

"And your friend! Wow what a great guy. What's his name, the sheriff or something?"

"Marshall."

"Great guy. Great guy. Fixed me up good. And no charge!"

"Yeah well he owed me a haircut."

"Yep he said that. Also said you owed him now and would have to take him dancing again."

I made a queasy smile and was about to explain to Blinks that I wasn't gay when I was interrupted by my cell. It was H.F.H.R. – Helen from Human Resources. "Yeah Helen, I would enjoy spending Saturday with you at the crafts fair, but I gotta come clean. I've gotten back with my girlfriend. I'm really sorry... Hell no, don't say that, you're not repulsive to men... I swear... I, I, are you crying Helen? C'mon, stop, please, any man would be overjoyed to take you out... 'Who?' Well I was talking hypothetically." Okay this had gone far enough. I had to find this poor woman a man.

"Hey pal, you want some?" I glanced over and saw the newly coifed Blinks offering me the half-eaten zeppole I'd tossed in the trash. Suddenly I felt an evil rise up in me that I didn't know existed. Dare I?

I had to get H.F.H.R. off my back so I fixed her up on a date with "a good friend of mine." Okay, okay, think of me what you will, but I had a lot on my mind. I was trying to solve a murder and didn't need any distractions. Besides a man was a man and I'm sure Helen would be grateful for the company. Right?

As I walked home from the boardwalk my thoughts turned back to the case.I kept picturing Sissy pumping Kyle full of bullets in a mad rage. Was it because she found out he was gay? I couldn't even be sure she did find out. And even if she did, why would it matter? She certainly didn't seem to be in love with the guy. Was it just a matter of a spoiled rich girl's pride?

Kyle's phrase "a marriage of expediency" kept popping up. Yeah the marriage would be expedient for him; he was getting dough out of it and might have been plotting to get a whole lot more. But if she wasn't in it for love what would Sissy be getting out of the deal? Was it all a plan to keep Mommy happy by pretending to finally settle down? Did Sissy have to be married to get her hands on a trust fund or something? Or maybe Ariélle had simply had her fill of girls gone wild and was threatening to cut off Sissy's allowance altogether. Heaven forbid! The poor girl might be reduced to driving an American car!

216 PORK CHOPS OF DEATH

So the three major players were Kyle, Tammara and Sissy.
Were they all working some kind of scam together? If so
why did good ole Kyle end up a stiff? Of course there was a
fourth player, Kyle's roommate/lover Lucas Nash. Did jealousy
overcome him? Was Lucas the one who pumped Kyle full of
bullets?

Wait. How did I even know what Lucas was telling me was
the truth? Maybe it was more than a marriage of expediency.
Maybe Kyle was straight or bi and actually having an affair with
Sissy.

Damn! The pieces still didn't fit. All the evidence
pointed to the fact that Kyle and Sissy didn't have a sexual
relationship. You'd expect lovers to leave some evidence of
their presence. Yet there were no men's clothes in Sissy's hotel
room, no woman's clothes at Kyle's dump. In fact the only
thing I found that suggested sexual activity was... Marone! I
did it again. I broke my own rule. Never assume anything!

An hour later I was in the Babylon standing outside the
door to the room where Kyle was killed. With me were
Guadalupe the housekeeper, Tina the girlfriend, and Nicky
the four year old Tina was babysitting and couldn't leave
alone. Guadalupe was feeding from an open box of vanilla-
nut fudge I'd brought her from Berkeley's Candy Shop on the
boardwalk - the best fudge in the world incidentally.

"Zolly I don't like this," Tina said nervously. "Why do we
have to do all this sneaking around?"

"Because sneaking around is part of being a detective. Slowicki's not answering his phone and I need to see the murder scene right away."

"Murder?" Nicky asked, his innocent little eyes looking up at me fearfully.

"Nah, not real murder. Murder like in the movies, you know, like when somebody shot Bambi's mom."

"Somebody shot somebody's mom?!" the kid asked with alarm.

"Zolly!" Tina scolded.

"Here son have some fudge." I handed him a square from the box and his eyes lit up.

"His parents don't allow him to have sweets Zolly," Tina said. Then she whispered in my ear "You didn't say anything about murder. You know I get sick seeing blood. Remember what happened during the Red Cross blood drive?"

"It'll be okay there's no blood," I said wearily. "Hardly any. Well it's dried anyway," I added under my breath. Then I turned to Guadalupe. "Maybe after you open the door you could take the kid somewhere?" Guadalupe nodded, her mouth too full of fudge to answer.

"I want to go home," Nicky whined.

"Sure, we're all going home as soon as I take care of something real quick. In the meantime Guadalupe here is going to teach you about the hotel business. Have you ever wondered how they make that little point on the end of a roll of toilet paper?"

"I want to go home," the kid said louder. "I want to ..." I cut him off by offering another piece of fudge and he grabbed it eagerly. Guadalupe took the key card from around her neck and was moving it toward the electronic lock when suddenly the door across the hall opened. A rotund middle aged woman with brilliant red hair and rosy cheeks stepped out. Surprised to see the little convention taking place outside her door she eyed us warily.

"Good evening, Ma'am," I said, tipping my hat to her.

"Is everything all right? I heard the boy..."

"Fred Sims," I said, cutting her off and handing her a business card. "Babylon Guest Relations. We're having a little lock problem here. Is yours operating properly?"

"Yes I think so."

"I want to go home!" Nicky demanded. Instantly I grabbed a piece of fudge and stuffed it in his mouth. His eyes widened again, but I couldn't tell if it was from joy or I had cut off his air passage.

"Sure you do son, and we'll have you home in your room in just a moment."

"Are you sure everything is...?"

"And for you Ma'am," I jumped in. "I'd like you to have this complimentary coupon to our Tower of Babel Buffet to express our apologies for the disturbance."

"There we go," Guadalupe said, unlocking the door but opening it just a crack.

"Excellent," I told her. Then I turned to the red hued woman. "Do you require anything else, Ma'am?"

"No," she mumbled, staring at the coupon and turning back into her room as if I had just spun her around ten times.

As soon as her door closed Guadalupe led Nicky down the hall. He didn't seem inclined or physically able to resist.

"Does your Mommy use single or two-ply" she asked him. He mumbled something and chunks of vanilla-nut cascaded from his mouth.

I took Tina's hand and started into the room, but she planted her feet and yanked me back. "Zolly this is nuts!"

"I know, I know baby, but trust me. I know how to do my job."

"I want to go home!" Out of fudge I had to think quick.

"Okay look, you said you owed me big for taking you dancing didn't you?"

"Yeah I did. Are you calling that in?"

"Yes I am."

"Huh." She shrugged her shoulders. "I would of thought you'd have saved that for sex or something."

"Yeah me too," I said sadly.

"Well, what do you think?" I asked Tina after giving her time to go through the clothes in the drawers and closet. "You notice anything odd?"

Tina was admiring a short black beaded skirt jammed in between the other clothes in the closet.

"I don't see anything strange here Zol. Other than the fact these two women have real different clothes budgets. For the price of a skirt like this I could pay my rent for three months."

"Hold on." My eyes brightened. "Are you saying there are clothes here from *two* women?"

"Yeah. I think. There are two different sizes. Of course a lot of girls keep a separate 'fat' wardrobe."

A 'fat' wardrobe for Sissy would still be baggy on an anorexic. "But," Tina continued, showing me a beige tailored jacket a few hangers down. "Whoever wears this is shorter and a lot more broad shouldered. They couldn't be the same person."

Dammit! I'd looked at the women's clothes and just assumed they were all the same size. "I love you!" I shouted, hugging Tina and lifting her into the air. Other than the fact little Nicky would barf up fudge in the backseat of my Mini Cooper, it was a great night!

CHAPTER SEVENTEEN

The next morning I hung three more pine tree air fresheners in the Red Demon. The rear-view mirror was beginning to resemble the Black Forest. Then I called Ariélle and arranged a private meeting between just her, me and Sissy for that afternoon. Just as she had asked me to trust her that Tammara couldn't be involved with Kyle; I asked her to trust what I was about to do. I just might be getting to the bottom of the whole mess.

When I arrived at Ariélle's suite she let me in herself. She was wearing black stretch pants and a striped boat neck top. Now don't get the wrong idea, I'm not a guy who would know the names of women's clothing. It's just that once Tina caught me staring at a hot chick and I had to pretend it was because I liked the shirt she was wearing. Tina told me it was called a "boat neck."

As I glanced at Ariélle's breasts with nautical interest I couldn't help but come to the conclusion they hadn't dropped an inch in three decades. As I stood staring at the two magnificent globes I suddenly knew how Columbus must have

felt discovering the new world. Ah well. All hands on deck.
There was work to do.

Inside the suite Sissy was sitting on a sofa, legs tucked
under her, examining her face in a hand held mirror. "Does it
look like I'm about to break out? With all this stress I think I
may have slipped and had some dairy." Then a look of alarm
crossed her face. "You do think I'll be able to get soy milk in
prison don't you?"

The prison milk should be her biggest problem. Suddenly
I envisioned Sissy banging a tin cup against the bars of her
cell screaming "where's my *Vogue* you dirty screws?!"

"You are not going to prizon," Ariélle said like an empress
issuing a decree. She took the mirror from her daughter's
hand. "Give Mr. Michelangelo your attenzion."

She sat beside Sissy on the sofa and I began to talk to
them like a prosecutor addressing a jury. "What I'm about
to tell you contains both bad and good news, so please
let me finish before shooting the messenger." I looked at
Ariélle and took her stoic look as an okay. "After conducting
my investigation I believe I have solid evidence that your
manager, Tammara King, was involved romantically with
your daughter's fiancée, Kyle Broder."

"Mommy!" Sissy screeched, staring at her mother as if
asking for protection from the boogey man.

"I told you zhat wasn't possible," Ariélle said flatly.

"Please let me finish." I took a leather attaché case
from under my arm and unzipped it dramatically.

Watching all those TV lawyer shows had really polished my presentation. I wondered if actual lawyers ever acted like that, or if they got it all from watching the tube. Was anything real anymore?

"I have several eye witnesses who will testify to seeing Miss King and Broder together." I took a file out of the attaché, opened it, and handed it to Ariélle. "Unfortunately there's also an indisputable paper trail that proves King was skimming money from Aphrodite, Inc. and funneling it to Broder."

"This is so ridiculous!" Sissy sprang angrily off the sofa.

"Is Aphrodite your company, and were you aware of these payments to your future son-in-law?"

"Yes it iz, and no I wasn't," Ariélle answered, looking through the stack of photo-copied evidence.

"Mommy!"

"Sit," Ariélle said as if giving a command to a misbehaving dog. Sissy sat.

"And as you can see the checks were all signed by Tammara King."

"I don't know what to say," Ariélle said sadly.

"You can say it isn't true! You know Tammara wouldn't steal!" Sissy cried.

"The evidence is there. I'm sorry." I turned my back to Sissy so she wouldn't see the 'take one more step toward my trap' smirk on my face.

"It's all lies!" Sissy shouted.

"Is it?" I asked, pivoting on her. "Why would you defend a woman I just told you was screwing your fiancée?"

"Because I know it's not true. Because Tammara is my friend!"

My voice softened and became less confrontational. I spoke to Sissy now like a wise uncle giving advice. "Tammara is a good friend isn't she?"

"Yes," Sissy said, on the verge of tears.

"Is it possible she's more than a friend?"

"What are you talking about?" She gave me a look that could turn me to salt.

I walked to the double doors to the suite and opened one partially. Slowicki was there with a fist full of hangers holding women's clothing.

"Now?" he said. "Is Ariélle in there?" He tried looking past me into the room. "Is it true in private she walks around wearing nothing but high heels?"

"Yeah. And I got the heel marks all over my back to prove it." I grabbed one of the hangers from his hand, shut the door, and returned to Sissy on the sofa. "Do you recognize this blouse?" I flourished it before her.

"No I don't," she said, in her put-upon rich girl voice.

"You don't recognize it? That's funny because I got I got it out of your closet."

"He's going through my things now?! Mommy, will you please fire this pervert?!"

"Mr. Michelangelo what does zis hahve to do with anything?" Ariélle asked.

"I can see where you might not recognize the blouse because it isn't yours. It's not even your size is it?" I handed the blouse to her. She gave it a perfunctory glance.

"So what if it isn't?"

"I see." I nodded my head and went back to the foyer. As I opened the front door I was blinded by the flash of the camera Slowicki's arm was poking into the room.

"What was zhat?!" Ariélle asked, turning her head like an enraged T-Rex.

"Get the hell out of here!" I shouted, grabbing the rest of the clothes from Slowicki and slamming the door. "Damn paparazzi! They're like vultures. But I think I put the fear of God in him." I carried the handful of clothes over to the two women and started to show off each item one by one like a sales lady. "Is this one yours Sissy? How about this one?"

"None of those are mine."

"No, they all belong to a person who's a different size then you. So why did I find them in your closet?"

"I know zhat one," Ariélle said, pointing to a red cashmere sweater embroidered with a small golden koala bear. "I think I bought zhat as a birthday present for Tammara when we were in Sydney."

"Oh yeah, of course." Sissy leaned forward to take a closer look. "I remember now. I borrowed it from her."

"Really? I didn't take you for a koala kind of gal."Not that she wouldn't pin a live koala to her sweater if someone told her it was chic.

"Did you borrow *all* these clothes from Tammara, even though she's not your size?"

"What iz going on?" Ariélle stared in her daughter's eyes with a look of confusion and pain. "If you know somezing that could save you from prizon why aren't you telling me?"

"Go ahead Sissy," I said, the wise old uncle again. "Your mother loves you very much. Let her help you. Tell her."

"You know?!" Sissy asked, her shock being the first honest expression I'd ever seen on her face.

"I figured it out."

"You can tell Mommy," Ariélle said, gently taking Sissy's chin in her hand.

Sissy looked up to the ceiling as if praying for divine intervention. Her fingers dug into the arm of the sofa and her shoulders arched tensely. "Tammara and Kyle couldn't be lovers... because Tammara is gay." Sissy's lips remained parted as if there was more to say but the words had evaporated as they passed through her mouth.

Ariélle's face was frozen granite. She stared at Sissy several moments before speaking. "I know zhat. I've known zhat for years but never thought it was anybody's business."

"But there's more isn't there Sissy?" I prodded. Sissy had turned her back to us, relieved that the worst was over, but my words caused her to snap around and shoot daggers at me.

"Tell me," Ariélle commanded. Sissy's eyes darted to her mother's face and she blurted out the secret she had kept bottled up so long.

"Tammara wasn't Kyle's lover... She's mine."

The two women stared at each other as if it were a single frozen frame of a movie. Then a deflated Sissy collapsed against the sofa back. She covered her face with her hands and made an impossibly long sigh. Along with that breath she seemed to exhale a lifelong agony.

Ariélle retained her granite pose, but I could see tears welling in her eyes and her lips begin to tremble. That's when something amazing happened, something so simple and yet profound. Something only a mother could do. Ariélle reached out and gripped her daughter's knee. A grip that said "I am here, I will always be here."

"I love you," she said.

"Oh Mommy I love you too!" Sissy's body was shuddering with sobs. The two women lurched into a hug. "Oh God how could I tell you? How could I dare let anyone know? Can you imagine if the press learned the woman voted sexiest female in the universe had a lesbian daughter?!"

"What would I care?" Ariélle shook her head in regret over all the fear and dread her child had had been forced to live with, and the insignificance of what anyone else in the world might think of either of them.

I cleared my throat to let them know I was still there.
"So this whole engagement thing, it was a 'marriage of
expediency?'"

Sissy looked at me suddenly realizing her trial wasn't
over, there were a lot of questions still needing answers.
"For years Mommy begged me to settle down. I knew I
was causing her pain, but how could I settle down? How
could I find the right person when I wasn't even looking
for the right sex? Then by some miracle I fell in love with
Tammara. But I couldn't even tell anyone! It's so unfair. I
hate being me!"

Ariélle put her hand on her daughter's cheek. "Baby, you
have to learn to expect unfairness and be pleasantly surprised
when you don't find it."

"I wanted to be with my love, and yet I had to protect
Mommy. So what if the thing with Kyle was all fake. People
were forcing me to live a lie, why not lie back?"

"A marriage of expediency," I said again and Sissy nodded.

"I knew Kyle's lover had a lot of medical bills and needed
help. Don't you see? Everybody was going to be helped. And
nobody was going to get hurt. Nobody."

"Only someone did get hurt," I said, the prosecutor again.

Sissy made a frustrated sigh. "At first Kyle was thrilled to
dig himself out from under the bills. But then I noticed he
was blowing some of the money on stuff like clothes and a
car. Can you imagine anyone so shallow?"

I had to fight hard not to bite my tongue on that one. But Sissy didn't notice. As usual she was oblivious to anyone but herself and continued her complaint. "Pretty soon Kyle was spending money he didn't have. Which is why you shouldn't give money to poor people - they just don't know how to handle it. Anyway, he kept squeezing us for more and more and Tammara was getting scared that she wouldn't be able to hide the money she was borrowing from Mommy's accounts. So she decided to call his bluff and tell him he'd only get what we'd agreed to and not a penny more. How could he be so stupid to risk such a good thing?"

"It's always a bad idea to bet on somebody being smarter than they are greedy. Kyle wasn't and it cost him didn't it?" It was a dumb thing to say to her. Her body closed in on itself and she retreated to the deepest corner of the sofa. When it looked like Sissy wasn't going to say another word Ariélle moved close to her.

"We need to know everyzing baby. Please." It was one of the few times in her life Ariélle begged for anything and Sissy recognized it. After a deep breath she turned to us, shaking with dread.

"I called Kyle to my room that morning to tell him he'd have to go back to our original deal or get nothing!" Her eyes rolled back as the scene replayed in her head. "He went ballistic! He called me a selfish bitch who wanted to keep all Mommy's money for myself. He warned that one way or another he was going to get his share. Either I paid or he'd sell the tabloids the story of the sex queen's lesbian daughter!"

I put my hand on Sissy's shoulder and tried to help pull her up out of the deep hole into which she'd fallen. "You were crazy with fear, in a panic. He was screaming at you, maybe even pushing you around. Without thinking your instincts took over and you defended yourself." Sissy's eyes opened. She rose to her feet and moved quickly to the window, turning away from us.

"Kyle went for the phone on the table and started dialing. He was calling this pig reporter, the same lowlife who printed all those horrible things when Daddy died. Who said Mommy killed Daddy!"

"Oh my God." Ariélle's body contorted as if the accusations were blades stabbing her midsection. Sissy turned sharply to face us.

"I had to stop him! I looked around the room for something to throw - a lamp, a chair - my eyes fell on the nightstand by the bed. The gun! I remembered there was a gun in the nightstand! I ran and tore open the drawer, I felt the cold steel in my hand, I waved it at Kyle and warned him to put down the phone! But he wouldn't. He wouldn't put down the damn phone and... I shot!" Her body convulsed with each imagined explosion. "Shot! Shot! Shot! Until my arm ached. Then I tossed the gun on the floor and walked out of the hotel into the street. I didn't know where I was going but I knew I had to keep walking.

I walked and walked, trying to get the images of what I had done out of my head, but they wouldn't go away! I had to make them go away!" After nearly screaming Sissy became quiet again. "I don't know when or even if I made the decision, but there was only way to get the images out of my head. I had to share them with someone. So when I saw the police cars parked outside the station, I walked in."

"You were out of your head. People will understand you didn't mean to do it," I said.

"No! I wanted to do it! I hated Kyle for what he was doing to me. For what he was going to do to Mommy. I was sick of going through life with somebody's hands around my throat. Sick of worrying about the one slip, the one mistake that would make those hands strangle the life out of me. If anyone was going to die it was Kyle. I wanted him dead. I wanted his hands off my throat!" Sissy's hands flailed at the air and her knees buckled. "Please," she begged. "Please let me pay for what I've done and leave Mommy out of this!" With an explosion of tears she wrapped her arms around herself as if to keep her body from flying apart and fled up the spiral staircase.

CHAPTER EIGHTEEN

I stood gaping at the spot where Sissy disappeared as my brain struggled to catch up with what had just happened. Then, remembering Ariélle was still with me; I turned and found her staring into space like someone who had just witnessed a horrible car wreck. I walked over to her and said "I'm sorry. I'm sorry that's not what you wanted to hear."

Ariélle's eyes turned down to the floor. "Yes. And if I hadn't hired you we might never have known zee truth. I was certain my little girl was incapable of murder. But all I've accomplished iz to supply zee police with a perfect motive."

"You did what you thought was right to save her."

Ariélle suddenly looked up at me as if having an epiphany. "But we can still zave her. We can claim it was a crime of pazzion. Kyle told her he was breaking off zee engagement because of another woman."

A new energy filled Ariélle. She sprang off the sofa and strode across the room putting together the pieces of her plan. "Zey argued. It got heated. Like you said, he started pushing her around. Threatened, she remembered zee gun in zee nightstand and grabbed it to defend herself. Zey struggled over the gun. Maybe Sissy isn't even zee one who pulled the trigger! I have zee best lawyers Zahlee. At zee very least we can claim temporary insanity, get her off on a reduced charge. My God! Anyzing that doesn't end her life."

"There's only one problem with that Ariélle. I know the truth."

"But you don't hahve to tell anyone. Don't you see? What harm will it do? Kyle iz dead and nothing iz going to bring him back. Iz a lie a lie if no one knows, if no one iz hurt?"

"I'm sorry, but a man is dead. Somebody has to be accountable for that."

Ariélle sighed and spun away from me in frustration. She stood with her back to me without speaking for a very long time. Then I could see her shoulders tense as she made a very difficult decision. "I am not a woman without means Mr. Michelangelo. I could make zings very comfortable for you."

"Please Ariélle, don't insult me and yourself. Nothing would please me more than to make you happy. If I could do this for you I would without asking for a thing. But I don't play that way."

After another pause Ariélle turned to me with a coy smile. "Of course you don't. You're a good man." She moved to me and rested her hands on my shoulders. "I apologize."

"That isn't necessary. I understand how you feel and my heart goes out to you."

She nodded slightly and her hands slid along my shoulders and moved upward. I felt her long cool long fingers wrap around the back of my warm neck. A shudder rippled down my spine. "I wish I had met a man like you sooner Zahlee. My life might have turned out so differently."

"A-Ariélle," I stuttered. Her head tilted toward me, her face mere inches from my own. My God what a face! The epitome of feminine grace and beauty, it had the saintly aura of a Joan of Arc and the sultry leer of a Salome. It was the face filling a magazine I had held over me so many times as a fourteen year old on my wagon wheel bed. Suddenly I was transported out of place and time to a world of shadow and fog existing somewhere between dream and reality. Ariélle and I were floating on a fluffy white cloud in a blue heaven.

"I have spent my life chazing zee illusion of happiness," she whispered, the words slithering sensuously through pursed lips. I have squandered my affectionz on handsome, powerful, virile men - while zee entire time my soul was yearning for someone like you." Her lips drew within millimeters of my ear and her warm moist breath licked inside, igniting a million nerve endings.

The sensation was so intense my eyes closed. Miniature versions of me dressed as Cupid spun in circles around my head.

"Po-zess me," Ariélle murmured, moving her mouth closer and closer to mine until our lips were within an atom's width of touching. My eyes opened and stared into hers. Those eyes! Amber jewels with flames of lust dancing wildly in each dark pupil. At that moment I knew how the gazelle feels staring into the eyes of the lioness about to devour him. And I didn't care. I welcomed the sublime puncture of canines ripping through my flesh. I ached to be dragged by the neck to her den.

Our lips touched and I felt a thousand red hot ingots pulse through my veins - threatening to explode through every square inch of my skin. I was the rare man in a hundred million who was actually living out the most cherished fantasy of his entire life. Ariélle was mine! My body vibrated like a tuning fork and felt like it was about to burst into a billion pieces, freeing my soul at last to escape to Paradise.

But no! Dammit! No! Another feeling churned deep within. A feeling drilled into me by a hundred raps on the knuckles from ruler wielding nuns. A feeling implanted in my chest like a pacemaker by parents, teachers, priests, coaches, scout masters, and even the sappy TV sit-coms I was weaned on! There it laid buried deep in my breast, watching and waiting vigilantly to strike at any moment I was in danger of experiencing pure raw pleasure! The pacemaker of guilt!!!

It released a corrosive poison that ate at my guts as it screamed "Do the right thing Zolly! Do the right thing!"

"No. No!" I gasped, startling both myself and Ariélle. "I can't do this."

"You can. You know you want to."

"That's the understatement of the century," I shouted, pulling my lips from hers. "Oh Damn! Oh shit!" I stomped around the room trying to shake it off.

"Forget your stupid ethics Zahlee. Do you think anyone cares?! Do you think anyone else plays by those rules?!"

"Yeah. At least one," I said quietly. "Tina does."

"Tina?"

"My girlfriend."

"You hahve a girlfriend?!" she asked incredulously.

Hey she didn't have to say it with such surprise. Even the beast in *Beauty in the Beast* found someone to love him. And he had hooves.

"I didn't know Zahlee," Ariélle said contritely. "Zhat night at my show you zaid you didn't hahve anyone in your life."

"I would have said anything to keep you on my lap kissing me. I would have given the Big Bad Wolf a map to my grandma's house."

Ariélle moved to the large sliding glass doors and stared out at the horizon. "Do you realize my life iz over?!" she shouted, throwing her body against the plate glass as if trying to jump through it.

"My god, I had no idea you felt like that. I swear if Tina ever comes to her senses and dumps me I'm yours in a second."

"AHHHHHHHHHH" she screamed in frustration, throwing her arms in the air. "God iz so cruel only giving penises to creatures without brains."

"I'm sorry. I know you were talking about your daughter. It's just that testosterone has a way of temporarily numbing brain cells."

Ariélle turned to me again and was a different person. The spirit or soul or whatever you want to call it, the thing that inhabits a bag of bones and transforms it into a human being – was gone. It was like turning off a light bulb. "My life iz over."

"Ariélle I'm sorry. I'm really sorry. I wish there was something I could do."

"You don't *hahve* to do anyzing. You don't have to say anyzing. Please Zahlee."

I shook my head sadly. "I'm sorry."

It was at that moment I witnessed firsthand the inner strength and pure determination that had created and sustained the rare creature known as Ariélle. She was a fighter. Recognizing momentary defeat her mind immediately shifted into a new gear. Her face changed from sorrow to defiance. "Then I'll tell zee police zhat I shot Kyle!" she declared.

"What?"

"I'll tell zee police I killed Kyle for harming my daughter."

"That's crazy."

"But it's true Zolly. You don't know zee lengths I would go to to spare her."

"The police will know you're lying."

"What? Do you think I'm not capable of murder when someone has wronged me? Don't you remember all zee rumors about my husband's car crash? I can tell you zere are still many people who believe I killed him."

I looked at her in a new light. Was the angel of my dreams an angel of death? "Did you kill him?" I asked, my mouth suddenly dry.

Ariélle shuddered and her face became stone. "All zhat is necessary iz for people to believe I could have."

I didn't press her further, maybe because I really didn't want to know the truth. "You must really love that kid," is all I could think to say.

"I have no husband. I have no friends whose loyalty could be counted on if zey weren't on my payroll. And in a few years when the skills of a plastic surgeon are no longer able to maintain zee illusion of 'Ariélle,' I will most likely have no fans. Sissy iz all I hahve Zahlee."

"Stop it! You're not going to help Sissy by throwing away your own life."

"This will work. Zee police have nothing other zan what Sissy told zem. I'll get her to change her story even if I have to have her committed!"

"They have a corpse. They have a gun."

"Yes a gun registered to me and with no fingerprints because I wiped zem clean in a desperate attempt to cover up what I'd done. Zere's no proof who held that gun."

She was right. Like a lot of things about this case it always bothered me that the gun had no prints on it. Sissy admitted to wiping them off, but only after seeming surprised to learn that someone had. No the pieces never fit. Something was always missing.

"I am going to do zis Zahlee."

"And I'm going to tell the police what I know."

"It won't matter what you *think* happened. Only two people were in zhat room – Kyle and his murderer. He won't be talking but I will."

Two people. TWO people… or THREE? Of course! It was so damn obvious, how could I have missed it?

I spun around so quickly it startled Ariélle. "Look. You've gotta trust me. Don't say anything to the cops until I get back. Keep Sissy with you and don't let her talk to anyone!"

CHAPTER NINETEEN

I tore down two flights of stairs before realizing I was out of my mind; then took the elevator the rest of the way down to the fifth floor. This was the floor where Guadalupe usually worked and I was praying I'd find her. Luck was with me. I spotted a maid's cart parked in front of an open door and rushed in shouting "Guadalupe!" I heard a frightened gasp and turned to see an old geezer in a bathrobe in the doorway to the john. Paralyzed by shock he stood as motionless as a statue. Drops of turquoise toothpaste dripped onto his chest from the toothbrush protruding from his mouth, creating a sort of Southwestern style necklace.

I made the serious mistake of allowing my eyes do drift down and discovered that the top half of his robe wasn't the only part spread wide open. For a moment I became a character out of King Lear, imploring the Gods to pluck out my eyes.

Then the old geezer stumbled forward a couple inches, his withered muscles unable to hold his stance. Thank God he was still breathing. I whipped a business card out of my blazer pocket and waved it past his eyes so fast it would be impossible to read even if he could find his reading glasses. "George Thomopoulos, Hotel Security," I barked sternly. "We've had numerous complaints about thefts from our rooms. Please keep your door closed and locked at all times." With that I dashed out into the hall, closing the door behind me and hoping for the best. I didn't read any obits for old guys dying of shock over the next few days so I figured I was in the clear.

"Mr. Zolly, jou want something?" I turned and saw Guadalupe coming out of the room across the hall with an armful of dirty towels.

"Guadalupe I need to talk to you." I rushed her back into the room.

"What did jou bring me to eat?" she asked. At least I think that's what she said. The TV was on in the room and made it hard to hear her. I walked over and turned down the volume.

"I didn't bring you anything but I'll owe you a sausage sandwich, okay?"

"I guess so, just remember, extra peepers."

"Extra peepers, you got it. Now listen, you're sure you saw a woman with a black scarf and dark glasses coming out of 652 the day of the murder?"

"Jes. I swear to Santa Isadora that's the truth."

"Okay great. And have you been thinking about what time it was when you saw this woman? Was it around eleven o'clock when the police think Kyle was murdered?"

"I would really like to help jou, even though jou didn't bring me nothing. But I really can't remember Mr. Zolly. I'm sorry."

"Damn!" I muttered, unable to hide my disappointment. I knew who did Broder in, but I had no way to prove the killer's presence at the time of the shooting. Seeing a mystery woman come out of 652 without being able to establish it was anywhere near the time of the shooting left a big gap in my theory. I'd just have to hope the gap wasn't too wide for a jury to leap across and come up with a conviction. But to have any chance at all I'd need Guadalupe to make a sacrifice. "Listen Guadalupe, I've gotta ask you something and it's very serious."

"Santa Cecilia, I don't like the sound of this."

I explained to Guadalupe that I needed her to testify in court that the day of Kyle Broder's murder she saw a woman in dark glasses and a scarf wrapped around her head leaving the murder scene. I explained to her that this would mean revealing how she had filled in for her friend who had to take her granddaughter to the dentist. And how her boss might very likely discover she had done this behind his back without permission. I promised her that I and Ariélle would do everything in our power to prevent the boss with the steak up his ass from firing her, but that I couldn't guarantee one hundred per cent she wouldn't lose her job.

Guadalupe gave me a solemn look and nodded. "Of course I will do this Mr. Zolly. If I didn't how could I ever again ask Santa Maria to help me?"

I was genuinely touched. It was rare moment to find a person who actually put their religion where their mouth was. I told Guadalupe she was a good woman. She thanked me and asked when she was going to have to go to court. I explained I wasn't sure how this was all going to turn out. I had a pretty good hunch who killed Kyle Broder, but I was a little light on proof. It wasn't a sure thing she'd ever be called on to testify. I told her I'd keep her updated, and in the meantime if she remembered anything about the day of the murder to give me a call.

"I will Mr. Zolly. And don't jou forget the extra peepers."

"Okay." I turned and walked quietly for the door, mulling over my next move. Behind my back Guadalupe reached for the volume control on the TV and an explosion rocked the room.

"BAM!"

Guadalupe's shout rang in my ears like a cannon blast, its impact stopping me in my tracks and arching my spine. Before I could gather my thoughts I was assaulted by another "BAM!"

"What the hell? What's wrong?!" I turned to see her staring up at the TV screen, her face beaming.

"BAM!"

"Look Guadalupe, I'll bring you extra extra peepers if you'll stop doing that."

"Mr. Zolly look the TV!"

I gave the TV screen a perfunctory glance. "So?"

"The cook show is on. The cook who scares the mierda out of you by all of a sudden shouting 'Bam!' I mean you're not even expecting it. Nobody in my neighborhood comes up behind jou and yells 'Bam!' It would be their last 'Bam.'"

"I'm glad you enjoy it." Confused by her zeal I started out again.

"Stop. And don't be so cow-headed!" Guadalupe called after me.

"Cow-headed?" I figured it out before her glare burnt a permanent mark on my face. "You mean 'bull-headed?'"

"Whatever jou says."

"The phrase is 'bull' headed."

"Is a bull more stubborn than a cow?"

"How do I know?"

"Jou don't know but still you are sticking to it. Jou are so cow-headed."

"Are you trying to tell me something? "Jessssss," she said making a long frustrated hiss like a radiator. "It reminds me. The chef show. It was the same show that was on the day the murder happen. BAM!!!"

"Would you please stop that?!"

"I know. I know Mr. Zolly when I saw the woman with the scarf come out of 652!"

"You do?? How?!"

"That morning I was watching TV while I was cleaning like I always do. And when I see the lady come out of 652, the BAM chef was making pork chops!" Her face lit up proudly as if she had just told me the secret to the universe.

"And the BAM chef is on every day at...?"

"At eleven o'clock!" she shouted.

"And witnesses say they heard gun shots around Eleven. So if you saw the mystery woman come out of 652 while the chef was cooking pork chops, it means you saw her come out right around the time the shots were fired! Guadalupe 1 could kiss you!"

Caught off guard Guadalupe stepped back and threw up her hands. "Jour a nice man Mr. Zolly, but I'm not the kind who kisses someone just because they feed me."

CHAPTER TWENTY

On my way back upstairs I called Ariélle on my cell and told her what we needed to do. When I arrived at her suite her face was as solemn as a statue on Easter Island. And that was the cheeriest welcome I'd get. The room was slightly less festive than a wake. Sissy was sitting on the sofa. Well you couldn't actually say she was sitting because her body was in constant motion, fidgeting one way, shifting another. Her eyes were bloodshot from crying and a white handkerchief in her hand trembled like an Aspen in the breeze.

At the closer end of the long sofa Tammara King balanced on the edge of the cushion as if it were a diving board and she were poised to leap. The pit bull seemed restrained by an invisible leash held tight in Ariélle's hand, but I could see in her eyes that if it weren't for Sissy's sake she would have pounced for my neck and torn out my jugular. I never liked big dogs and was feeling a tad uncomfortable.

As soon as Sissy saw me enter the room she jumped to her feet and shouted "I am not going to put up with this little man's bullshit any longer!"

Little man? Boy did I know some prison guards I'd like to introduce her to.

"Sit!" Ariélle commanded and Sissy sat. Now I had two angry wolves watching my every move, saliva dripping from their jowls as they could almost taste my blood. Well it goes with the business. I wasn't there to get elected prom king.

I paced back and forth in front of the sofa like it was a jury box, trying to choose my words carefully so as not to inflame the situation further. Not yet at least.

"So," I said with a pained frown. "I'm supposing you've already told Tammara that the secret of her relationship with Sissy is out."

"I hate you!" Sissy shrieked. And I swore I could hear Tammara growl but I might just have been the acid churning in my gut.

"There's no need to yell," I said. "All I'm trying to do is get to the truth. Personally I could give a shit what you people do in your private lives." And that was the truth. I couldn't understand what the big fuss was over two women getting married. To me it was a good idea. Let a chick find out what it's like being married to a chick. We men have carried the burden too long.

"This is absurd!" Tammara snapped, turning her glare on Ariélle standing at the opposite end of the sofa beside Sissy. "What purpose can my presence possibly serve, other than being a target for more of your insults?"

"You will be quiet!" Ariélle's terse warning shot through the air like an icy spear. I could see she was restraining herself for Sissy's benefit. I'm sure in her heart she wanted to lash out at the woman who had taken her daughter from her. But Ariélle knew this was not the time. Not with Sissy's life literally in the balance.

"What? Are you going to fire me twice? There's nothing you can do to me Ariélle. I love your daughter and nothing will ever change that. Do you think you're the only one here losing their love?"

"You truly do love her don't you?" I asked, stopping my pacing in front of Tammara. I wanted to put a hand on her shoulder to express my compassion, but I also wanted to keep all my fingers.

"Of course I do." She looked up at me mournfully, some of the anger in her eyes replaced by sorrow.

"Everybody loves Sissy. So let's all work together to do our best for her." I moved to Sissy at the other end of the sofa. "I want you to tell me everything that happened the morning Kyle was shot."

"No! I'm not going through all that again. Tammara and I are in love, but it changes nothing. I shot Kyle. I killed him!"

"Stop saying zhat!" Ariélle shouted.

"It's true Mommy, it's true."

"Are you sure?" I asked.

"Ohhhhh!" she screamed in frustration. "Mommy why are you letting him torture me like this?"

"Maybe because she wants to save you from spending the rest of your life in prison," I said. "Have you really thought about what that means? No Mommy, no Tammara, no friends. No Beverly Hills mansion with its maids and cooks. No Mercedes Benz. No designer clothes. No traveling to the latest hot resort on a whim. Can you picture spending the rest of your life in a six by ten concrete box? Can you?"

"Zahlee please!" Ariélle pleaded soulfully, placing her hands over the searing pain in her stomach. Sissy's jaws parted to scream, but nothing came out. Instead her body shook and imploded like one of those buildings you see taken down with explosives. Only in those implosions nothing's left but a cloud of dust, and in this one it was a cloud of tears. I felt like a real shitheel but somebody had to finally say this to the kid. Somebody had to make her face what was really at stake here.

"I want to help you Sissy. But I need you to tell me exactly what happened in that room."

Sissy looked as if she didn't believe anything could help her, but that it would be quicker and less painful to answer my questions. She spoke with as little emotion as a court reporter reading back a transcript. "I told you. Kyle demanded more money and we decided to call his bluff."

"And what was your plan if he didn't come around?"

"We didn't have one. I guess we were bluffing."

"So you didn't go into the meeting thinking if Kyle gave you any trouble you would threaten him with the gun in the nightstand?"

"No! Of course not. It didn't start out like that."

"But he did call your bluff didn't he?"

"Yes. I never saw him so angry. He was a wild man. Like somebody on drugs!"

"Only the drug he was addicted to was your mother's money." I always say you never knew the true character of a person until they've faced temptation.

"He was dialing the phone, he was going to talk to that creep reporter and destroy Mommy! I didn't know what to do; my whole world was crashing down around me like I was in a giant earthquake. I looked around. I saw the nightstand. I remembered the gun. I only wanted to scare him. I swear. I begged him to put down the phone. Please Kyle, put down the phone!"

"But he didn't."

"So I pulled the trigger. It was loud and it hurt but I pulled the trigger over and over and over!"

"Did you walk over to him and shoot?"

"No. I, I was by the nightstand."

"And Kyle was across the room using the phone on the table by the window."

"Yes," Sissy said, her eyes searching mine for some clue as to what I was driving at.

"You stood across the room and fired wildly, your hand jumping from the recoil, your shoulder aching."

"Yes."

"The forensic evidence shows you *were* firing wildly because the room was sprayed with bullets. One broke a lamp, another shattered a TV screen a good six feet away from Kyle. Bullets were dug out of the ceiling and carpet. And of the bullets to hit Kyle one barely grazed his thigh and another passed through his forearm. But that's where the poor bastard's luck ran out. The third bullet got him right in the heart."

Sissy wailed. "Please... Don't!"

"Please," Ariélle implored. Tammara sat like an ice sculpture, her eyes boring into me.

"You unloaded the gun?" I asked after a few moments for us all to catch our breath.

"Yes."

"You counted every shot you took. Bam! One. Bam! Two!"

"Of course not! Why would I? Who would...?"

"The police report says all six bullets were fired. But forget that for a minute. Tell me what happened next. Did Kyle fall?"

"Oh God," Sissy moaned. "He slumped down onto one knee. He was so shocked. You can't imagine the look in his eyes!"

"Was he still holding the phone?"

"Yes."

"So you didn't hang it up?"

"No. I didn't think about doing anything like that. I felt sick. I felt like I was going to have a heart attack. I just shot a man!"

"And what did you do next?"

"I threw the gun on the floor and ran out."

"Wait a second. You told me before that you wiped your prints off the gun, then threw it on the floor. Which one is the truth?"

A new shock wave hit Sissy and her head recoiled from me to her mother to the floor.

"Which one is true, Sissy?"

"Tell him baby," Ariélle implored. Sissy's eyes flashed to her mother.

"It's alright Sissy you don't have to worry about implicating your mother. Your mother didn't come into the room and wipe the prints off the gun, isn't that right Ariélle?"

"God knows I would have if I'd known. But my baby didn't come to me. Zee one time in her life when she needed me zee most she didn't come to me! I didn't know anything until zee police knocked on my door."

"You didn't hang up the phone and you didn't wipe the gun clean, did you Sissy?"

"No...no... I didn't. I ran. I just ran."

"And there's something else you didn't do Sissy. You weren't counting the shots so you couldn't have known, but you didn't empty the gun. There was one bullet left in the chamber."

"Are you sure?!" Ariélle asked, shocked out of her sorrow and glimpsing the faintest glimmer of hope. I went on.

"The last bullet in the gun wasn't fired by an amateur. It was fired by a person familiar with firearms, perhaps from their military training. And the last bullet wasn't fired wildly from across the room but at close range right to the heart to insure it would be fatal."

"Oh my God!" Sissy yelped.

"It was fired by the same person seen walking away from the scene of the crime by the maid cleaning a room down the hall. Walking calmly, not running."

"Zahlee?" Ariélle asked, stunned by the puzzle she was piecing together in her mind.

I stepped along the sofa and stopped before Tammara. "Just a few minutes ago you told us how much you love Sissy. Did you really mean it?"

"Of course I meant it," Tammara answered from inside a fog that had suddenly engulfed her.

"Then why would you let her take a murder rap for you?"

"Tammara?! What is he talking about?!" Sissy asked, her brow contorting from the extreme effort her brain was making to keep up.

"Do you really think she could do the time easier than you?" I continued, searching Tammara's eyes.

"You bitch!" Ariélle screamed. She lunged for Tammara but I grabbed her and held her back. "How could you do zis to my baby?!"

"Mommy! Stop. Please!" Sissy pleaded.

Tammara turned to face Sissy. "Oh Baby I'm so sorry. I swear I don't know how it got this far. I was in shock. I was scared… scared for us. All I wanted was for us to be together. I thought without any prints on the gun and no witnesses… that with your mother's money… it would never get this far. Celebrities don't go to prison. It doesn't happen!"

Marone. I'd had my fill of the modern judicial system, and more than my fill of the selfishness of human beings. Maybe we'd all be better off if we had some nasty old nuns to rap our knuckles with a ruler once and awhile. Enlightenment wasn't all it was cracked up to be.

"I don't understand," Sissy groaned from her cocoon of confusion. "Is he saying Tammara had something to do with Kyle's death?"

"Oh Sissy! I should have been there with you!" Tammara cried. Then she turned to me as if I were her confessor. "I was supposed to be there with Sissy when she told Kyle we weren't going to give him any more than we'd agreed on. But Ariélle had some stupid problem with her costumer and wouldn't let me go and by time I got to Sissy's room thing's had already gone horribly horribly wrong."

"You were wearing a black scarf and dark glasses, isn't that right?"

"Yes. It was something I copied from Ariélle, and used to fool the paparazzi. I always dressed like that when I was with Sissy. We were very discrete, but if they should catch us they'd automatically think I was Ariélle. It was deliciously perfect."

Now if I were a psychiatrist I might have read something into Sissy dating a woman who dressed up like her mother. Luckily I'm not so I asked Tammara to go with her story.

"I used my key to enter the room. It was like stepping into a nightmare. The kind where you know it's a nightmare but you can't force yourself to wake up. Kyle was alone. He was down on his knees, his hands pressed over the wound oozing blood on his thigh. His eyes were wild with shock and he was screaming incredulously: 'That bitch shot me! Can you believe it?! That bitch shot me!'"

"You see? I shot him. I shot him!" Sissy repeated, still not getting it. But what could you expect from a kid with an I.Q. slightly above asparagus?

"Then what happened," I asked Tammara, ignoring the vegetable.

"Kyle kept screaming. 'That bitch shot me! Call an ambulance! For God's sake what are you waiting for call an ambulance Tammara!' And the telephone kept screaming. It was making that frantic hideous 'phone off the hook' electronic clanging. It pounded my eardrums like a single key on a piano hit over and over. My head began to throb. My eyes searched the room and spotted the phone receiver dangling off the edge of the table on its coiled cord. I sleepwalked to it thinking 'call an ambulance. I've got to call an ambulance.'"

"'Oh Jesus it hurts!' Kyle groaned. 'That stupid bitch and her mother are really going to pay now. The papers are going to piss themselves bidding for this story. You bitches thought you could keep Kyle quiet? Well he just hit the lottery baby!'"

"Kyle's words slapped me across the face. I stared at the phone receiver," Tammara continued, sleepwalking now as in her story. "All I could see was our lives being flushed down a drain. All I could think of was being parted from Sissy. And all because of this greedy worthless bastard. What right did he have to ruin our lives? Whatever happened he brought on himself."

"What did happen?"

"Using my skirt as a glove I hung up the phone. One irritation had been dealt with, another waited. Kyle watched me and continued shouting: 'What the hell are you doing?! Call an ambulance bitch!' Stupid, greedy Kyle. He never knew when to stop overplaying his hand. I crossed the room, picked the gun up off the floor by the nightstand and came back to him. Oh yeah. The insults stopped then. The cocky arrogance in his face was quickly replaced with fear. He tried to stand but was too weak."

In her mind Tammara stared into Kyle's face for several long moments until I pulled her back to the present. "And then?"

"And then," she said in a steely voice lacking even an ounce of regret or remorse. "And then I did what I had to do to protect my love."

"You fired the last remaining bullet into his chest."

"Yes," she answered, almost proudly.

"My God," Ariélle gasped, covering her face with her hands.

"Then you wiped the gun clean and walked away from a dying man as calmly as if you'd just emptied trash into a dumpster."

"He was trash. He didn't deserve better."

"I can't believe this Tammara! Are you saying you killed Kyle?!" Sissy stared at her lover and her mouth fell open. I wouldn't bet on this chick in a lightning round.

"Cold blooded murder," Ariélle said, her eyes shooting barbs into Tammara. "In all our years together I never would have believed you were capable of zis. It makes me shudder to zink how many times I was alone in zee same room with you." Ariélle closed her arms over her chest as if to contain a sudden chill. Tammara turned on her with a look of disdain.

"Oh please Ariélle, spare me the fake shock and 'holier than thou' bullshit. It's nothing you wouldn't have done. In fact it's exactly what you did to your own husband."

"Tammara! No. Don't talk to Mommy like that," Sissy pleaded. Ariélle unfolded her arms. Her voice was hoarse but the look of strength returned to her eyes.

"If you are using me as an excuse for your behavior you are making a very bad mistake. I won't lie. My marriage to Eric was a catastrophe and his death uncomplicated my life, but I am not a murderer. Eric accumulated gambling debts faster zhan I could pay zem. A lot of zee wrong people were very angry with him, and at least one didn't share my qualms about taking a life."

"Ariélle why didn't you tell anyone? Why did you let them slander you?" I asked.

"Because my daughter didn't need to hear any more bad zings about the father she was already mourning. I decided to let zem think what zey wanted. In a way it was even helpful. It was a warning I was not a perzon to be taken advantage of."

Ariélle's revelation seemed to take the air out of Tammara. The pit bull was a German Shepherd now. Okay I'll cut her a break – an angry Collie. But she remained defiant and convinced she had done the right thing.

"What I did, I did for our love," she said to Sissy across the room. "My only regret is hurting you baby. Can you forgive me?"

"Of course I can!" Sissy shrieked, running to embrace Tammara. Now I'd like to tell you I'm not like a lot of guys who get off seeing two women kiss so I averted my eyes. I'd like to tell you that. But you know me too well by now. Besides I'm a student of human nature and this was a part of my education.

When the two of them were finally able to pull themselves apart I felt Tammara's eyes on my skin. Her voice was softer now, almost pleading. "If you've ever been in love you'll understand Mr. Michelangelo."

"I've been in love plenty," I said. "But I'd never be able to enjoy that love if it came at the expense of another person's life." Then still curious about something I added: "Or should I say the lives of *two* people?"

"Two Zahlee? What do you mean?" Ariélle asked.

"Ariélle when I asked you not to tell anyone about J-Up's blackmail threats, you went ahead and told Tammara anyway, didn't you?"

"I'm sorry Zahlee. If zere was one perzon in this world I thought I could trust it was Tammara."

"Two?" Sissy asked. Her brain was an abandoned train station where thoughts whizzed by but never stopped.

I turned to Tammara. "You took J-Up's threats seriously. You were afraid he was going to tell Ariélle his suspicions that Sissy was gay. Isn't that right?"

"He walked in on us once at the beach house," Tammara said weakly.

"The beach house in Avalon?" I was feeling cocky and wanted to show off my investigative prowess.

"Yes, the same house you followed me to when I went to meet Sissy. We tried to hide Sissy by slipping her out in our friend's hoodie, but I guess you figured out we made the switch."

"That's right," I said, lying through my teeth. I had no idea at that time that Sissy was the lover Tammara was meeting at the love nest. Or that they had snuck Sissy out past my eagle eye wearing the hoodie. But why disillusion them by tarnishing my image as the super detective? Tammara continued in blissful ignorance.

" When J-Up walked in on us in bed, we told him Sissy wanted to surprise him with a threesome. Either his hormones overpowered his anger, or his ego wouldn't allow him to accept the fact the love of his life was a lesbian, so he believed us."

"Some people are so stupid," Sissy sighed. I immediately pictured an Uncle Sam recruiting poster with Sissy in a dunce cap saying "I want you!"

"The question is..." I said to Tammara. "When you gave J-Up the drugs were you hoping to simply buy his silence, or did you know they were so pure they'd shut him up permanently?"

"I can't believe it!" Ariélle stared at Tammara now as if looking at a monster.

"No!" Tammara answered. "I only gave him money. I'm not responsible for what he did with it."

"Yeah if that's what you want to believe," I said.

"Oh Mommy. This is so horrible!" Sissy ran to her mother and wrapped her arms around her. "I'm so sorry."

Ariélle looked into her daughter's eyes. "Don't you know zere's nothing you could have told me zhat would make me stop loving you?"

"So what happens now?" Tammara asked. Her eyes were laden with sorrow but flickered nervously with the smallest hope that I was the kind of person sympathy or money could persuade to remain silent. I had to disappoint her.

"I think it's time to talk to the cops," I said.

Tammara closed her eyes to the world, perhaps forever.

"And Sissy? What happens to my daughter Zahlee?"

"Well she didn't kill anybody like she thought, but there is the little matter of attempted murder, or attempted manslaughter. I'm betting by time it's over your lawyers will have plea bargained it down to jaywalking."

"Oh Mommy!" Sissy squealed. "Is it true? Is it?"

Ariélle held her daughter and stroked her hair to assure her. "Mommy will do everything in her power to see no one harms you."

"No Mommy, I mean, do you think your lawyers are good enough get Tammara off?"

If ever there was a time to say it this was the time: "Marone!"

EPILOG

Oh yeah this was living. Cuban salsa played on the boom box as gentle ocean breezes wafted over my body. To the good life! I lifted my glass in a toast and sipped my Mai Tai as the sun set between my feet at the end of my chaise. I was king! The chaise was my throne and my second story porch the balcony from which I addressed the multitudes coming to seek help and wisdom. Okay maybe not multitudes at this moment; just a couple of horny teenagers making out against a car and a well coiffed Blinks scurrying stealthily down the street with a plastic lawn flamingo tucked under his arm. I'd deal with him on the morrow. Tonight was reserved for the celebration of my victory!

Things turned out pretty well if I have to say so myself. True I violated my cardinal rule 'never assume anything' a couple of times; but sometimes you get lucky. Like when I found that strap-on device in the drawer in Sissy's room at the Babylon. It didn't make sense at first why a chick and her fiancée would be in need of something like that, unless the guy was in the top three percentile of kinky. No this was the kind of toy usually enjoyed by two women. Bingo! Sissy and Tammara. They were a couple! When you start down a road you never know where it's gonna lead you.

"Freshen up your drink baby?" Tina appeared beside me with a pitcher of Mai Tai's, wearing the sarong I had requested.

"Certainly," I replied, and heeding the King's every command she began to pour. "Ooh wait!" I said, springing up urgently.

"What Zol? What's wrong?"

"You've got something on your face I don't like the looks of. This could be serious."

"Oh God Zolly what is it?!"

"Hold still baby." I took her face in my hand and examined it from several angles. "I think it's, it's..."

"What?!"

"A smile!" I leaned in and planted a big kiss on her cheek.

"You are terrible!" Tina said, giggling and trying to pull away. "Let me go or supper's going to burn."

"Let it!" I pulled her back and kissed her again as the track on the CD changed to something faster. "Mambo!" I shouted, grabbing Tina's hand and dancing her around the porch. Even the kids making out against the car looked up at us with envy. As my feet maneuvered each intricate step I kept thinking how proud Dot the dance teacher would be.

"Zolly you're a dancing fool," Tina said, ignoring the crush of my foot on her big toe. The cell phone in my pocket began to ring but I ignored it. "Answer your phone silly." Tina broke free and hurried inside the apartment. I smiled after her, intoxicated by the heavenly scent of her perfume – or it might have been the aroma of home cooking wafting out of the kitchen.

"Hello?" I said, answering the persistent cell phone. "Helen!" Oh God it was the call I had been dreading ever since I momentarily lost my mind and fixed H.F.H.R. up on a date. Was she going to call me a shitheel? Would there be outrage and threats of lawsuits? Would she wail in agony and question how I could do this to another human being? What kind of pond scum was I?

"Zolly you had your chance with me and you blew it," Helen said. Somehow she seemed more coy than angry. Was it possible that after the atrocity I had committed she was still flirting with me? Good lord this was one very lonely woman.

"Wh-what?" I stammered with great eloquence.

"That's right Zolly. After fixing me up with your friend I can't imagine ever dating another man."

Oh God. I had become Shiva, destroyer of worlds. H.F.H.R.'s world at least. I'd put her off men forever!

"Zolly I thank you from the bottom of my heart. Detective Sowicki is a dreamboat. God bless you." Helen hung up and I dashed to the porch railing to search the sky for an impending comet about to destroy the earth. Surely this was a sign of the apocalypse. Slowicki a dreamboat? What *kind* of nightmares had Helen experienced to come to that conclusion?

"Look what I got," Tina said proudly as she set a tray of food on our small patio table. "They smell great Zolly. What put you in the mood for pork chops?"

"Well babe I was watching one of those TV cooking shows and the chef had this recipe for killer pork chops. I thought to myself 'Tina's such an amazing cook I bet she can make those even better!'"

"Oh Zol, you're the greatest!" Tina gushed, throwing her arms around me. We were about to tangle tongues just as my cell phone rang again. Crap! Was there no way to stop Helen from calling?

"Hello," I said in a voice tinged with annoyance and sexual frustration.

"Iz this a bad time Zahlee?" Ariélle asked. The phone almost leapt out of my hand.

"No, no, of course not." I covered the phone with my hand and told Tina it was important business. "What can I do for you?" I asked, hurrying inside my apartment.

"Zahlee I didn't want to leave zings between us zee way zey are."

"What way is that?" I began to feel a tingle in my gut. Was it possible my relationship with Ariélle could be more than business? Had my sharp mind and dazzling display of fancy detective work attracted her to a man who was let's say, a bit off the mark from her usual type?

"Everyzing happened so fast the last time I saw you, I didn't have zee opportunity to tell you how eternally grateful I am."

"Oh? Well I understand, things got crazy at the end there, but I appreciate hearing it." Was I beginning to sweat?

"Zahlee I need to find a way to show you my gratitude."

"Ah heck that's not necessary Ariélle." My mind began to flood with images collected since the onset of puberty.

"But it izz Zahlee. I cannot go on without thanking you for giving me back my child. You have made me complete again. Zere must be somezing I can do to repay you. Somezing I can do to complete you."

Complete me?! Ariélle was offering to complete me! This was a life transforming moment. A moment you tell your grandchildren about on your death bed. I had to choose wisely. "Ariélle there is something you could do that would make me very happy." My voice was barely audible over the pounding of my heart.

"Anything Zahlee."

"Could we, I mean, could you... find the hottest dance club in town ... and get me and my girlfriend in?"

"Of course Zahlee." Her voice was full of disappointment. "But you are not being fair. You are leaving me with a great debt. Surely zere is somezing more. Somezing you hahve always yearned for.... Hello? Zahlee are you still there?"

"Okay, okay, there is one thing." My Hawaiian shirt was drenched with perspiration as if I'd been in a rain storm.

"Ariélle, I have to confess that you have been my obsession since I was a young man. It was you who taught me the rich complexity of desire. I was a dumb kid then, but all these years later I am still hypnotized by your enigmatic beauty. After all these years the obsession continues. And in your words, there is something you could do to complete me."

"Tell me Zahlee," Ariélle whispered in the dusky sultry voice that held all the great mysteries of the world.

My hand gripped the phone tight enough to crack the plastic as I summoned up courage from the depths of my being. "Ariélle I ask one thing."

"Anyzing Zahlee. It iz yours."

"Where were you born?"

There was a silence longer than an arctic night and then that voice returned with the last word that would ever be spoken between us:

"Brooklyn."

THE END